Crazy Days

Crazy Days

A Book of Short Tales

James Howerton

iUniverse, Inc.
Bloomington

Crazy Days
A Book of Short Tales

iUniverse books may be ordered through booksellers or by contacting:

iUniverse
1663 Liberty Drive
Bloomington, IN 47403
www.iuniverse.com
1-800-Authors (1-800-288-4677)

ISBN: 978-1-4759-6841-5 (sc)
ISBN: 978-1-4759-6842-2 (ebk)

Library of Congress Control Number: 2013901871

Printed in the United States of America

iUniverse rev. date: 01/30/2013

Cliffords Leg...

"Dad, this is a mistake," Clifford said.

"No, Cliff. Believe me, this is the best way the leg can be tested."

His father was a lovable but mad genius, and prone to disastrous ideas about how to test a robotic prototype. That was no doubt why Clifford's mother had left them so many years ago.

"The best way— no. Football? Our practice football, but not real football."

"We've come this far, Son."

We've come this far, Clifford thought, knowing it would finally arrive here.

Dr. Kensington glanced over and smiled from the steering wheel of the Volvo that was approaching Clifford's high school. They could see the football players out there on the muddy field. It was a wind-wet day. Greasy Nebraska clouds doomed the sky.

"If this is a mistake," his father said. "Then why did you work so hard to help me build the leg?"

"I don't know. Because you're my dad."

1

Clifford stared in dread at the football players out there on the Plainview High School field. Tough jocks who'd elbowed him and pushed him away in the hall; now in brutal armor. He stared at the twin monuments at either end of the sodden field, the straight-up tuning forks that marked the end zone. The Uprights. Simple steel monuments, more holy than Stonehenge.

"Why, Clifford?"

"So that somebody who lost a leg might get one back," Clifford said to the end-posts. "So that our leg could be more than about kicking field goals."

"Good answer!" Dr. Kensington laughed at his son. "But a lot of B.S. It's time to cut the crap, Cliff: You always dreamed of playing football."

Clifford looked over. "I'm skinny, Dad. I'm fairly weak. I'm very smart, but I'm no athlete. I don't have physical powers."

"You do now."

His father pulled the car into the high school parking lot. When the old man got an idea into his brain it was impossible to get it out, no matter how insane it was. Dad wanted more than recognition for what he had done, he needed glory. What better place to earn it than the gladiatorial spectacle of football?

Clifford was seventeen years old and could stop this thing. But then he looked out at the gloomy mist of the football field where the players were practicing to fight for glory. Like Dad, he needed glory.

They got out of the Volvo, and Dr. Kensington checked his hand-held computer. "It's programmed," he said. "How does it feel?"

"Like a part of me." Clifford rubbed the super-graphite leg that tingled against his thigh. He wore a pair of electro-magnetically charged football pants. The robot leg they had crafted in the garage in some demented father-son project, made him proud, but fearful: Dad handled the composition, fluids and engineering; Clifford handled the electronics and computer messages. A leg for a war veteran or a traffic accident. Something more than a stump or a plastic can-opener. Months of crafting this thing, this robot that was now attached to his puny leg, walking with him toward the football field. They had designed it so well that only a close inspection would reveal it to be anything but a normal, if heavily muscled, right leg.

"Prosthetics will go far beyond just replacing lost limbs," his father lectured him for the hundredth time. "We can now make better arms and legs than nature. And by Gumbo, we're going to prove it!"

Clifford followed his father into the wet, dismal day. He could hear Coach Wall bellowing at the football team, the mighty mud-blood-stained soldiers in plastic armor.

"You Do want to prove it, Clifford." His father stopped him and gave him a look. "Because if you don't . . ."

"I guess so." He smiled at his father: "Yes, I do."

"For the girl." His father's eyes sparkled. "That girl who lives down the street from us."

"Sandy Pendleton? Dad, she's a cheerleader. She's like Ambercrombie and Fitch."

"So? You're going to be the hero of the day. How's your data connection?"

Clifford read the tiny screen hidden under his wrist sleeve. "It's good. Dad, this is one of your mistakes."

"No it isn't, Clifford. She's a babe."

"Who?"

"This Sandy girl. When you become a hero."

"Dad, I'm never going to be a hero. Let's just publish our data, and—"

"In the Journal of Prosthetic Surgery. No, that would be about as spectacular as nothing. This is more than some plastic replacement leg, and I won't have it advertised that way. This was a Six Million Dollar Man achievement, and you worked very hard, Cliff, and I'm very proud. But now something spectacular has to be done. A hero has to be made. Seize the day, my son, and you might seize the cheerleader. Make an engineering and medical breakthrough in the lab, and scientists might ooh and ahh—the rest of the public will yawn. But perform a miracle on the football field, and the whole country will be stunned!"

It was the P.T. Barnum side of his father that had finally chased Clifford's mother away: His crazy ideas that only wound up embarrassing everybody. His eyes when they got that way, seeing glory. And also his eerie knack of reading his son's mind:

"Look how shamelessly Thomas Edison advertised," he said. "He once electrocuted an elephant!"

"I know he did, Dad."

"Well, my son, you have to decide now."

Clifford stared into the stormy day. He thought of Sandy Pendelton; he thought of the football men, those who'd punched him in the hallway. He plunged into the madness, having nothing to lose:

"Okay, let's try it, Dad."

"Very good." Dr. Kensington grabbed a handful of his son's shoulder and pulled him toward the coach of the football team. "Remember this, Clifford:

Henceforth you are the star of this team. Remember the cheerleader."

"Sandy Pendleton is dating the first string quarterback."

"Well, statistically a great field goal kicker is a more potent offensive weapon than a quarterback. Just do it the way you did it in our tests. Don't be intimidated."

(What?)

Coach Wall looked at them as they approached him. He was a glaring, impatient man; a walking muscle who chewed gum and blinked his eyes. He wore a rain slicker; a silver whistle dripped rain down his neck: "Yeah?"

"My son kicks field goals," Dr. Kensington said out of the mist.

Coach Wall sized-up Clifford. "Yeah, I've seen you in gym class," he said. "Craig Kenny. Two pull-ups?"

"Clifford, Sir. Clifford Kensington."

"Okay. I remember the two pull-ups."

"He has small arms, but a very good leg," Dr. Kensington said. "Football games are won with legs, not arms. Hence the name foot ball."

Coach Wall blinked at the grey Nebraska sky, the rain. He looked at the father; then he again sized up the son. A wobbly boy, likely to be snapped in two on the field. He looked down at the boy's legs. One was a lot bigger than the other. "How far can you kick?"

"Forty-five yards," said Dr. Kensington. "Right down the center."

"Excuse me, Sir, but I wasn't asking you." Coach Wall stared at Clifford. "How far can you really kick the football, son?"

"Fifty-five yards," Clifford said. "Right down the center. In the rain."

The coach guffed out a humorless laugh. A rumble of thunder followed that, echoing across the football field. The sky finally let loose, and he stood watching the rain pour down on Clifford and the old man. "I already have a field goal kicker."

"Can he kick in the rain?" the old man asked.

"He kicks pretty good."

Clifford stared into the rain, at the players in armor fighting in wet mud, grunting, yelling, cussing, bellowing, lining up to smash the other guy. He thought of Sandy Pendleton, and how she was a popular cheerleader, but not stuck up—no snob. She talked to you and cared about you. She was sweet and intelligent—and so beautiful.

"Give me one kick," Clifford said.

Coach Wall stared into his eyes. "Okay. One kick."

"And I want the defense to try their best to stop it."

Coach Wall looked at the boy's father. "How much does this boy weigh?"

"163 pounds," Clifford said. "You were talking to me, Sir."

"I'm not going to risk getting you hurt, Son."

"I'll kick the field goal from wherever you say, Coach," Clifford said. He looked at his father. "And no disrespect, Sir, but I'm His son." He felt the rain finally showering this grey Nebraska evening. "But I won't kick it unless the defense tries to stop it. Really tries to stop it; as if it were win or lose."

The coach studied him, but only for a moment. "Hey, get this guy suited up!" he yelled to a student assistant, Mike Meyer, who led Clifford into the locker room.

"Damn this sucks!" Meyer grabbed a towel and wiped the rain from his face. "Cliff, what the hell are you doing?"

"I'm trying out for the team. Here, get me suited up, Meyer."

"Those guys will break you to pieces. What do you think you're going to do out there?"

"I'm going to kick a field goal."

"You're crazy," Meyer said. "You're going to get crushed. What's that thing?"

"Nothing, just a watch."

Clifford checked the tiny computer screen on his wrist; then covered it with an athletic wristband. He rubbed at the graphite leg, felt the sparkling electric signals, the need to explode.

"No, don't touch the leg, Meyer. I'll keep these pants."

"What do you mean?"

"No pads on this leg. These are my lucky pants."

"The coach isn't going to like that."

"If all goes according to plan, he's not even going to remember it."

Clifford sought to distract him: "Why do you want to be the towel boy for the football team?"

"What?" Meyer's face was hurt. "I'm helping the team out."

"I'm sorry. That was a cruel and stupid thing to say."

"Okay. You go out there, Cliff, and you're going to make another fool of yourself. Only this time you might get really hurt doing it. Yeah, I'm a wimp like you, okay.

I'm the Team Assistant, and I get to go on the buses and watch the games and talk to the cheerleaders. I get to be a part of it, and I do my part to see that the team wins. But going out there on that field is another thing."

"I hope so."

Clifford stood, suited up and trotted into the rain. The coach was explaining to the defense that a really scrawny field goal kicker was being tried out, and he could hear some of them laughing when they saw him sloshing onto the field. Coach Wall looked at the kid's old man, sitting patiently in the rain, smiling and nodding.

I've seen your kind plenty. You want your boy to be tested on the field, okay. I've seen plenty of fathers like you, wanting to push your round son into a square hole. Then he gets hurt.

But there was something: What the father had said about field goal kickers, and how a time would come when they could win or lose a game. They were a wicked and hateful weapon. They died sometimes, in misery and defeat. Sometimes they made the death-stab, and all glory was to them. A species disrespected by their own team mates: a pampered, protected little mouse with a leg trots like a movie star onto the field, to decide life or death with a simple kick. No mud or blood on his uniform. Coach Wall had heard the old tired phrase: "A field goal kicker ain't a football player; he's a field goal kicker."

But the old man was right.

"Set the ball at thirty yards," Coach Wall called out. "Let's get this over with. Fourth and twelve. This is the game, win it or lose it. Block like monsters and give this kid a chance. This young man is going to try a field goal."

Clifford lined up, as he had practiced with his father many times in the back pasture. He stared through the rain at the holy tuning fork, the uprights that stood out of the grey distance. He told himself that if the leg worked as it had in so many tests, he would have to do essentially nothing. The leg would do it all.

So soon it happened: a wall of mud-stained barbarians exploded at him. The ball was snapped: Clifford trotted up and smashed it, feeling the death-mass dissolve around him suddenly. The football spun perfectly between the uprights. It was as simple as a shot in a video game, and Clifford stared over at his father, who was cheering and clapping from the sidelines.

Coach Wall trotted out and clapped him on the back. "Not bad in the rain," he said.

Clifford looked at him: "Let me do fifty yards," he said, grinning out of the helmet.

"Okay." The coach smiled and shook his head. He didn't want to see this scrawny kid hurt; but the scrawny kid had just drilled one thirty yards like a bullet through the rain. "You do that, Clark, and you're the field goal kicker."

"It's Clifford, Sir."

The defense set themselves against him, the giant high school linemen who'd despised him as a worm. Now they wondered about him. Clifford stared at the line of players. He slid the wristband down and made a quick check of the computer on his arm. He stared at the misty holy tuning fork at the end of the mud field one hundred fifty feet away. His robot leg tingled.

The ball was snapped, and he ran forward and aced it, shooting it like a NASA rocket straight between the uprights. Clifford looked over at his father.

It works, Dr. Kennsington thought. Our leg is more powerful than a leg.

Coach Wall ran onto the field. His eyes were mystified: "You're on the team," he said.

"I'm not really a football player," Clifford said to her.

Sandy Pendleton smiled up at him. They were in her parent's garage. It was getting dark; the fluorescent light in the garage glowed in the slow darkness.

He had stopped by to see her. She was making a mask for a Halloween party that he, of course, was not invited to. That didn't seem to mind Sandy Pendleton. It was a cougar mask, brown and black, with ivory-white fangs made of plastic.

Dusk fell over the trees. The garage light seemed like a soft island in the neighborhood gloom. Sandy Pendleton smiled up and put the cougar mask to her face. "Argggh!" she growled at him.

Clifford smiled. "I might get to kick—at the game this Friday."

"I hope you do," Sandy said. "Do you think you'll kick a field goal?"

"I might." Clifford said to her. "That's a great mask."

"It's important to make a good mask for a Halloween party—isn't it?"

"I guess so."

"It's important to make a good mask—isn't it?" Sandy Pendleton studied him for a long while: "It's important to kick a ball through the uprights."

"I'm not sure," Clifford said.

"You're not sure?" Dr. Kensington said. "Cliff, you're about to play in your first high school football game—on the varsity! You're about to test our leg on the most dramatic stage in America."

"A high school football game? Dad, this is cheating."

"So? If cheating is winning, then it's not cheating—it's winning."

"No, it isn't. Dad, if I play in this game, I might have to go out there and kick a field goal. With a robotic leg that—"

"Clifford, shut up!" Dr. Kensington gave his son a dry frown. "You can choose to go out there and play football, or you can choose not to. Choose one or the other, only don't snivel about it like some Saint Augustine."

"It's cheating, Dad."

"No! It is not. I've studied the rules of high school football, and nothing prohibits a player with a prosthetic limb from kicking field goals."

Clifford smiled at the old man. Crazy, brilliant, needing something really big to announce his super-robotic leg: a graphite leg, lighter and more powerful than any natural leg; connected by micro filaments to the nerves of his own leg. A tube filled with computer intestines of wire and silicon. A device that could kick a football so hard, at level ten, that it would explode.

"I'll give you glory, Dad, if I get the chance," Clifford said.

"No, don't give me anything: Take your own glory."

Clifford watched her dance and cheerlead, Sandy Pendleton, so beautiful and perfect. The game was a brutal contest, Plainview crushing themselves against the Rose Titans. Clifford sat in his clean, unbloodied football uniform and waited, somehow knowing it would come. The Plainview Wildcats were down by two. He studied the defensive line of the Rose Titans.

Clifford saw destiny crawl toward him as the giant clock in the end zone ticked away.

A time-monster crawled toward him. The fourth quarter was dying down to seconds. Plainview tried for a third and twelve and got stopped at the line of scrimmage.

Fifty-six yards for a field goal. Now was the Sandy Pendleton moment: He stood up from the bench and put his helmet on. He trotted up to the coach. "I can do it," he said.

Coach Wall studied him, the lost game making his eyes blink. "It's fifty-six yards, Clark. That'd be a state high school record."

"I know. And it's fourth and twelve. I can make this kick," Clifford said.

"That'd be one unbelievable kick."

"It's the best chance we've got to win this game." Clifford looked at the sidelines, where Sandy Pendleton was sitting, her cheerleader skirt blooming over her legs like a flower.

"That's fifty-six yards," Coach Wall said.

"If the line gives me protection, I'll make the kick."

The time out was nearly over. His quarterback and wide receiver begged him to order a Hail Mary. Coach Wall had to make a decision, and then face defeat and ridicule. He sent out the field goal team.

"Coach, give me this last play!" his quarterback pleaded. "Let me throw the Hail Mary."

"I'm the Coach. And I'm the one to throw the Hail Mary."

"How can you let that skinny wimp try and make a 56 yard field goal?"

"I've seen him do it."

Clifford lined up and stared away at the goal post, a distant doorway surrounded by infinite space. Voices roared out from far away. His mother's distant voice called out from a long-ago abandonment. Everyone watched the clock and breathed at this last-second try at victory.

The ball was snapped. Clifford trotted into the kick and the graphite robot leg sent it fifty-six yards into the sky and straight through the uprights.

The world exploded. Giant football players jumped on him, hugging him, crushing him to the ground. Astounded gasps and screams seemed to roar out of the night. Clifford wriggled out of the madness and grinned at Sandy Pendleton, who was rushing onto the field. Clifford stood and gave her a hug. "We won it!" he said to her.

"You won it."

"I don't believe this!" Clifford stared at the sidelines, where his father stood, giving him a bitter-sweet smile.

"You did it!" he heard Meyer's voice screaming into his ear, as he was mobbed by giants in bloodied and muddy uniforms. Even the quarterback—Sandy's boyfriend—took his face mask affectionately and slammed his helmet, grinning at Clifford. All those hours and all the computer calculations, and listening to his father's tireless pep talks and never believing . . . now it was true.

"You won the game, Cliff!" Sandy's voice echoed in his helmet. He grinned back at her beautiful face.

"I did. I did. I did."

He rubbed at the graphite leg.

"It worked! My God, did you see it work, Dad? Dad."

The dark shadows of their laboratory betrayed robot things, carbon fiber models; a father-son project gone mad:

"Yes, I saw it work, Clifford. We did it."

"We did it, Dad! I set the state high school record!"

"You did, Clifford." The old man looked sad.

"Look what it did. It goes beyond any—Dad, what's wrong?"

"Nothing."

"Our leg won the game. It's going to be in every paper in the state, that I set the state record at the last second and won the game."

"I know it will." Dr. Kennsington looked at his son. "With that leg, you could land in the history books, Cliff."

"And I will."

Dr. Kennsington smiled at his son. "I saw you hugging the cheerleader, the girl down the block."

"Sandy. She hugged me. She said she wants to go out with me!"

"She's a babe, no doubt about that."

"And those letters, Dad! Notre Dame, Nebraska, Oklahoma. Every big football school in the country!"

"I know, Cliff."

"What the hell is wrong?"

Dr. Kennsington stared a long while at the workbench, where much of the computerized robot leg had been created. He seemed lost for a moment.

"Dad, what is this? I did everything you said, and I always thought it was a mistake. But it wildly succeeded. Isn't this what you wanted?"

"It's not what I expected."

Clifford stared at him. "What? You're the one who kept telling me that it couldn't fail. You're the one who had all that sod put in and who built those test uprights to convince me that it Would work. You're the one who put guts into me and saw that I would step out onto the field and make myself a hero. Those are your words. And you were right. I'm proud of you, Dad."

"I'm very proud of you, Clifford."

"But you don't look happy. Not what you expected? You're the Only one who expected it. And now I understand what you were teaching me."

"Do you?" Dr. Kennsington only stared at the workbench. He couldn't look at his son.

"Yes! I went out onto that field and I did something that astonished the whole state of Nebraska, the country! In the final seconds of the game, when my team had nothing to lose, I stepped out there and set a state field goal record to win the game. I never thought I could do it. But, Dad, I stepped out there and I did it."

"Did you?"

No matter. It was now to prepare for the State Championship game against the Crete Cardinals. Coach Wall drilled his soldiers relentlessly, the unlikely Plainview Wildcats playing for the state championship against the dominate Class B powerhouse in all of Nebraska. It went beyond his dreams.

But it was now to put together a strategy that might actually work. His defense was solid, that reassured him. But they were up against the Crete Cardinals. His coach's instinct told him that the Wildcats' only hope of victory was to be tied with Crete until the last seconds, when he could send his greatest weapon out to win the game. If they could manage to stay less than two points behind until the final seconds, and if they had the ball at fifty yards or so, the Plainview Wildcats would make history.

A good coach, preparing for a monumental game, has to organize his mind—even for Class B high school football. The defense, the offense, the kicking game, the special teams. The line, the running backs, the receivers. But always before a game like this, one small and skinny ghost always haunts his mind: the field goal kicker.

The Nebraska State Class B Championship Game was held at Memorial Stadium in Lincoln, and this day it seemed the veritable Coliseum of Rome, more people standing and cheering than anyone could imagine. The whole town of Plainview in the stands, and Clifford feeling their eyes on him.

The Plainview Wildcats lived up to their name: They scratched and surprised and attacked Crete, clawing their way—thanks to a brutally beat-up defense—into the final seconds of the fourth quarter. They sensed victory, and that made them believe. Clifford had already kicked two field goals with his magic leg, a 29 and 27-yarder, like cutting into butter.

He prayed for a chance to win this game, the score at 27 Crete and 25 Plainview. He looked at Sandy

Pendleton and she grinned at him and gave him a thumb's up. He looked over at his father, who sat on the sidelines with a strangely tragic look in his eyes.

Clifford slipped up his wristband and read the mini-computer. No problem. He opened his palms to his father, as if to ask, What's wrong?

Dr. Kensington smiled sadly at his son.

Destiny stood on the forty yard line, with only fifteen seconds on the clock. Crete had the ball, but they got greedy. Their running back tried too hard and fumbled, and suddenly Plainview, in the Championship Game, had a last chance: field position and the greatest field goal kicker in the state.

The next play ate up a full twelve seconds. Coach Wall called an outrageously gutsy pass to the middle, but it worked. The ball was in the middle of the field, it was a mere 20 yards from the uprights and there was but 3 seconds left on the clock. Now was the time.

This is what we worked for, Dad, Clifford thought as he trotted confidently onto the field, the crowd roaring insanely, sensing another miracle, one that would make Plainview a legend in Nebraska football lore. The bitter warfare, the broken teeth and sprained legs and blood all coming down to two seconds and a field goal kick.

The coach of the Crete Cardinals called a time-out, as Clifford and Coach Wall knew he would.

Trying to rattle me, Clifford thought with a smile. But he had never felt so calm, so confident. He grinned over at Sandy Pendleton, who stood looking at him. In the background were the thousands of people in the stands, roaring at the miracle that was about to happen.

All eyes were on him, and Clifford quickly slid up his wristband and read the computer. Perfect.

Before the time-out ended, he trotted over to his dad. "This is it!" he said.

"This is it, Clifford."

A sharp whistle. Now was the time. Clifford trotted onto the field under the roaring fans. Two seconds to go, and one easy field goal would win it for the Plainview Wildcats and Coach Wall. The quarterback knelt and looked at him. The center was down, ready to go.

"This is for everything, Cliff," said the quarterback.

"I know it is," Cliff said. "Just do your job and don't worry about the kick. Believe me, I'll make it."

The stadium went silent. The leg was in perfect sync with his body. Clifford shut out the crowd, the drama. It only mattered that he make this kick, and he knew he would. Center of the field, only twenty yards.

He saw the ball launch into the quarterback's hands and he stepped up and kicked, as he had so many times when they tested the leg, always perfect. This is it, Dad: I'm the great hero and Sandy Pendleton is mine.

But something was wrong. Clifford watched the football sail toward the goal post. Something was terribly wrong. It wasn't going straight as it should have, it veered off suddenly and missed the uprights by only six inches. He could not believe his eyes.

Cheers erupted in the stands, the Cardinal fans going wild. The game was over. The leg had missed the field goal. Oh God, Clifford thought. It's true, I'm not the hero. It failed, Dad. It failed, and after all this, I do come out the loser. A very great loser.

"You're not a loser, Clifford," Dr. Kennsington said. "You missed a field goal in a football game, that's all."

"That's all? Dad, that's everything. A twenty-yarder in the middle of the field under perfect conditions? In the final two seconds of the State Championship Game, when everything was on the line. Everything I ever wanted was right there, it was perfect. Then the damned Leg malfunctioned. I could have been—I could have had—Sandy. All those huge jocks giving me high-fives and slapping me on the back—now they only despise me."

"Clifford, it wasn't you who failed," Dr. Kennsington said. "And it wasn't the leg. The leg could have kicked that field goal 20 times out of 20. A hundred times out of a hundred. It was I who failed you."

Clifford stared at his father. "What are you saying?"

"I re-programmed the computer." Dr. Kennsington stared at the workbench. He couldn't look at his son. "I made it so that you would miss the field goal."

Clifford was stunned. "What? After all we did and dreamed of—and you destroyed it. Why?"

"Maybe someday you'll understand and forgive me."

"Forgive you? For ruining my life. Dad, how could you do something like that?"

"I pray that one day you'll understand. And forgive."

"I had the chance to be a hero. Now I'm a loser. When the moment came, I fell down—that's what people are going to say."

"I hope I didn't raise you to care about what people say."

"You were the one who talked me into doing that. Being some high school hero. You were the one who taught me to go onto the field and be a hero. I did that, and it felt good. For the first time in my life I felt powerful, I felt confident. For the first time in my loser life!"

"If you feel like a loser because you missed a field goal, then I failed as a father."

Clifford stared at his dad. "You programmed the leg so that it would miss the most important moment of my life. How could you do that?"

"The most important moment in your life, Clifford, might be when you see an amputee walk, or run, or even kick a field goal. Someone who truly has lost a leg. Hate me if you have to, my son; but sometimes a father's teachings can be painful."

Clifford stared at the workbench. "Well, there goes my date with Sandy."

"I don't know about that. If she wants to go on a date with you, I don't think a missed field goal is going to matter. If it does, then that should tell you something."

"I can't believe my own father would set me up like that, then sabotage me and—"

"I'm not sorry I did it, Clifford. But just the same, I hope you forgive me."

"Was it me, or was it the leg?"

"It was the leg and you. But now it's just you."

Clifford smiled at his father. How can you not forgive a mad scientist?

An Obscene But True Story...

I'm retired, but I do work part time at the convenience store in Denton, Nebraska. (To be honest, I took the job in order to get my dead, drunken ass off the couch and away from the t.v.; to force myself to shave, take a shower, put on the store uniform and actually go out to the cruel world).

It was a Sunday night in December. The wind chill was about four below zero; not unusual for a winter night in Nebraska. Only a little snow, but enough to whish into mini tornadoes that spun down the street. It's the wind here in Nebraska that bites into the soul. Sometimes in the spring it will touch you and smell of new grass and warm days and you will fall in love with it. In the fall it will let you taste how sweet death is.

Here, in a winter blizzard, the wind is only a wicked villain. I stared out of the store at the American flag over the Denton Post Office. The damn thing shivered and lashed, tortured by the gusty white wind. I stared at the snow tornadoes dancing down the street. How can I live in a place like this?

When you retire, aren't you supposed to move to someplace warm?

What I've told you so far is beside the point. It was only at that moment, when I was staring out at the awful snow wind, I wanted some relief. And at that moment Ed's pickup pulled into the store.

He's a crusty rancher—I warn you now— who drops the F word the way most of us say "and".

Ed grouched into the store, stomping snow off his boots, snow swirling suddenly inside the store, the wind attacking, wanting to get in. A wave of cold swept over me.

"God Damn it!" he said under a ridiculous stocking cap. He stomped over to the beer cooler.

"How's it going?" I asked him.

Ed looked at me. "I'm freezing my fuckin balls off and I'm fuckin pissed. Get me a can of Copenhagen wintergreen." He crept off his knees, stomped over and dumped a Busch Light 18 pack on the counter.

"What are you pissed about?"

It seems Ed is a member of the Cowboy Church, which is a Christian congregation that meets to worship every Sunday in a barn out on Old Cheney Road. The barn, donated by Earl Honvalez, symbolized the manger.

"The fuckin church won't pay to fuckin insulate and heat the barn. So, hey why the fuck don't worshippers show up?"

A rhetorical question.

"I asked the pastor why the church can't insulate and heat the barn so that folks can come on Sunday to fuckin worship without freezing their fuckin balls off.

He told me the church didn't have the funds to pay for that. I told him—hey, the church can send our fuckin funds out to Third World countries that hate our fuckin guts, but we can't insulate and heat the fuckin church? The pastor told me I wasn't on the Church Board, and I had no say in how church funds were spent. I looked at him and I said, Hey, fuck you, asshole."

Ed took his beer and chew and stomped into the wind-blistered night, and when I warmed up, I laughed for fifteen minutes. It could be that Jesus laughed too.

Rupert . . .

Yes, my name's Rupert, go ahead and laugh.

My name is Rupert, and dang it, I'm angry. I found out that Mr. Hansen gave Bo McCormick a larger Christmas bonus than me. Gol dang it, that's just not fair.

I had bigger numbers than Bo McCormick this year, and I clean up after myself while Bo McCormick leaves trash all over the office. Bo McCormick does not fill out his beginning-of-shift report when he should. Bo McCormick does not pay attention to the monthly inventory reports, nor does he perform his site surveys, which he Must Do at the beginning of his Shift. No, he sashays down the aisles, grinning at the sales girls and frowning at the stock boys.

Listen to me. Bo McCormick was not respectful to the customers. He neither greeted them with a smile, nor did he ask them if they'd found the item they wanted.

More often he greeted them with the F word and grabbed them as if they were friends and not customers.

Jeemany . . . he did not even fill out the required paperwork. And many times—many times—he had not worn his name tag.

Yet Mr. Hansen gave him the larger bonus. Bo McCormick, who does not—you know it as well as me—take his job seriously. And I don't believe he's even a true Christian, though he wears that cross on his neck.

I shouldn't go on so—but it was a darn shock to me. I had tried so gosh-darn hard, you have to know that. I had memorized the Company Policy Book, and I knew full well what a good employee should be, and what Bo McCormick was.

I could have survived his friendly grin, and his usage of obscene words around the customers . . . but not that Christmas Bonus. That was the H E double L of it!

I went up to his house that night, and gosh darn it when he answered the door I stabbed him several times in the heart. Golly, he deserved it. Don't you think? I mean, he did not even keep the shelves stocked. No, Bo McCormick left that to me, and then got credit for it. He did not provide good customer service.

I pulled out the knife and Bo McCormick's dead body dropped at my feet. I wiped the knife clean and dropped it on him. You didn't even fill out your shift change report.

Land Of A Trillion Cameras . . .

Her favorite color was black. She dressed in black jeans and black blouses, and wore a strange black veil-cape that seemed to swirl a shadow mist behind her as she passed. Her form was never still; even when she rested, the darkness swam round her. She had a dangerous need to flaunt herself in front of the cameras—to draw attention to herself, though her face was nearly always hidden behind the fluttering black veil.

She wore black fingerless gloves and black eye shadow and a spider ring. Her visible body was covered in tattoos and piercings. The cameras called her Pin Cushion, and she sneered at them. The cameras called her Goth Girl, and she sneered at them. She was attractive, and her face and expressions fascinated men. But she made herself too scary and bitchy to find some stupid romance. She was not attracted to men or women; she was attracted to no one. She seemed determined to despise life; and sometimes she got a plummeting sense in her stomach that it was quickly coming to an end. She wanted no human to know her or any part of her lonely and uneventful existence. She wanted no one to know her secret, but those who worked with her suspected: She could read the cameras.

Like her veil-cape, Cassandra flowed through life in a dark mist. She had enrolled at San Diego State, but the superficial syrup of academia had soon turned her off. It was a place where professors taught knowing they were in the cameras. Where classmates laughed at her and chittered in the eyes of the cameras.

She lived in an efficiency apartment just off El Cajon Boulevard, and most of her money went to the rent. She ate simple and cheap Paleofood: raw fruits and vegetables, unsalted mixed nuts. She did not want to, nor could she use her kitchen. She ate tuna out of the can after straining it.

One day she talked about the curse; she didn't know why.

She worked at one of the head shops on El Cajon Boulevard, where strange artists blinked in, and stoned wanderers and grey old hippies wanting a bong on the sly. All of them slinking and trying to hide from the cameras. Mickey Shaw worked next to her at the head shop. He was an energetic meercat of a guy who stumbled over life in a determined way. He was an on-again off-again student who got around on a skateboard. He was very intelligent and very unconfident. On camera he approached the comedy of a silent film, swiping back his hair, practicing a walk. Cassandra knew that Mickey was developing a crush on her, she didn't know why. Like everyone else, he had forgotten how to live life. Now it was how to perform life. To try and be human and happy knowing that always the cameras are on you.

Cassandra had a curse: She alone could read the cameras, she could read them as quickly and simply as breathing. She could blink a code with her eyes and the closest working camera jumped into her mind. Some of them had audio, and that was even more frightening. The cameras protected everyone; they watched everyone. They looked down from everywhere, regulating the moving landscape of humanity. They could pinpoint, triangulate, expose in much less than a second. They were always upon her, all-seeing eyes and all-knowing judgment.

That strange day she somehow needed to talk about it; in only one hour she had seen three well-dressed people wandering outside, talking to themselves. She gave Mickey a fond but droll look: "I keep my ass covered with my cape," she said.

It took him a second to react. "What?"

"So why are you always staring at it?"

He gave her a You Bitch look: "To see if it's actually down there, beyond the black fog?"

She had to smile. "Good answer."

Mickey jumped on the smile: "I'm not the creep you treat me as," he said. "Close, maybe. But I'll bet you're more perverted than me."

"You'd lose that bet."

Mickey smiled at himself. "I've lost a few bets. I'm betting that someday you're going to go out with me."

She raised her nose. "Go out with you. Is this the 1950's?"

"Okay I'll talk modern. You will hang out with me; at a restaurant or a movie, or the dog beach."

"I'm not as cruel as you think, Mickey. But I would use my fingers to barf myself before any of those things happened."

"Okay . . . not interested." Mickey frowned out the window at the boulevard. "At least you can tell me why you're so hateful."

She frowned at him, then looked away. "You wouldn't believe me."

"I might."

"No one believes. I have the power of truly knowing people."

"You pay attention to the cameras, big deal. Nobody cares about the cameras anymore."

"The cameras show me people as they are. You could never understand that kind of curse."

Mickey shrugged. "So how did you get that curse?"

She sighed; then gave him a cold look. "I'm not going to explain something to someone who will not believe. I'm tired of trying to explain things that people won't believe. It gets old."

"Bite my ass. You see me on camera, you read me on camera like you do everybody else. And you become the camera judge, the one who gets to see people as they really are. You can read the cameras, I know that. How does it make you feel?"

"Disgusted," she said. "Completely disgusted."

"I thought so," Mickey said. "It'd probably make me disgusted. So what is it about me that makes you disgusted?"

"You fear the cameras, and at the same time you love them."

"Doesn't everybody—except you?"

"We're all trapped, and none of us know it; not even those who operate the cameras. We went too far with the cameras and texting and Facebook and i-pods and cell phones and always being in contact. It's like someone with great and ancient powers once told me: we gave our privacy to the cameras; and by doing that, we inadvertently created a virus of the mind."

"The cameras have their purposes," Mickey said. "They keep people honest; they identify thieves and murderers. They make rapists and child-molesters think twice. They stop a lot of evil."

"Do they?"

"I think so. Why can't you just ignore them like everybody else?"

"Just so you know, Mick; every time you sneak into the back room to smoke a bowl, the cameras are watching you."

He frowned. "Maybe."

"Not maybe. There are at least three of them across the street looking at you right through the walls. This is a head shop."

"A smoke shop."

She gave him a sour look. "I know you're a pothead; the cameras know you're a pothead. You smoke a bowl at about 9:30 every morning; another at about eleven—"

"Okay! But they'll leave me alone as long as I don't flaunt it. You—I don't know why— like to flip them the finger. That's hating a system that's only trying to protect you; that's rebellion against the future; they don't like that."

"Good."

"And there's no reason for it. You might as well protest against cars and indoor plumbing. The way I see it, the cameras are there so that honest businessmen can protect themselves against bottom feeders. If you're not doing anything truly wrong, then you shouldn't worry about cameras watching you."

Cassandra trained her strange dark eyes out the storefront at sluggish El Cajon Boulevard. "They listen too. Most people don't know that or think about it. They see what you do and they also listen to what you say. They're listening to us right now."

"You're paranoid, Cass. When you say 'they', who precisely are you talking about? The CIA, the FBI? Some dark organization from the Twilight Zone?"

Why was she even trying to explain this to him? Maybe because Mickey was so bitter about his own life that he didn't fear pushing her buttons. Most people did.

"I don't know who 'they' are. No one knows. I only know my curse. That's why I am what I am."

"So tell me how you got the curse."

"Why should I tell you what you won't believe?"

"Why not?"

"I'm tired of telling people what they can't believe."

"So tell me anyway."

She fixed him with her eyes. They were dark eyes, but eyes that coveted something. "I grew up in a small town in rural Kentucky. We lived in the hills and woods, where old ways were still practiced; by those who just didn't know any better. I wandered the hills and hollers, pretending I was an elf princess with magical powers. It was a stupid time in my life when I could still dream."

"I've been there," Mickey said.

"I lived in a pretend world of birds and butterflies. One day I wandered too far; I came upon a cabin where an old ragged woman was skinning a rabbit she had trapped. She lived almost like an animal herself, without any modern things—she didn't even have running water. But she had powers, I knew it. I don't know where her powers came from. She said they came from a strange mushroom that grew on the slopes. She said that she could die or be killed like the rest of us, but only temporarily. I began visiting her, and I brought her food; apples I took from the orchards, wild asparagus, bread I baked with my mother."

"What was the old woman's name?"

"Her name was Zianna. She never spoke the word, but as I got to know her and listen to her words, I knew. I knew the word."

"What word?"

"Witch."

"Okay." Mickey was studying her.

Cassandra looked away. "Now laugh, Mickey. Laugh at me. Cassie has a mental illness. But I don't."

"I'm not laughing."

"One day Zianna asked me why I kept visiting her, what I wanted from her. I said that I wanted to have the power to know people. I wanted to get out of the hillbilly world, I wanted to move to California and become rich and successful. How better to do that, I asked Zianna, than to have the power to know people; to know their secrets, their weaknesses, their desires, their hidden shames. To know people, and they couldn't know me back. To have that power.

"Zianna handed me a strange mushroom. Her hand was bony and cold, with blue winding veins. She said that if I ate this thing I would have the power I wanted. And she said that if I ate this thing I would be forever cursed with this power. I didn't believe the mushroom would do anything; this was a crazy woman living in the deep woods, nothing more. At worst the mushroom would make me sick; but it wouldn't give me the power I wanted. So I ate the mushroom. And, as I thought, it didn't do anything. I felt nothing until I moved to California. As I traveled west, through cities like Phoenix, I began to read the cameras. Then I knew what the power was, and the curse. How could the witch know of cameras and modern technology?"

"I'll be honest, Cass: I don't believe in witches or magic."

"I know you don't. You like to get stoned and read science fiction books at night, in your lonely apartment. You also watch too much porn and you masturbate too much."

Mickey lost his balance momentarily. "I do not—"

"Yes you do. That's all right, most people do. It would astound you what people do when they think they're alone and not being seen. It would sadden you to know how lonely people are when they think they're hidden from the cameras. When they're not out on the streets performing for the cameras, many people are lonely and sad and perverted and disgusting. I can see it all; that's the curse the witch Zianna gave to me—the curse I took willingly. I wanted that power. I pretended that an old woman in a far Kentucky cabin could give it to me; a woman who said she had lived almost forever. And that I could become the elf princess I had dreamed of. That no one could hurt me, because I would know them, down to the bones of their souls. The mushroom gave me the strange ability to read the cameras, something I never could have dreamed of. Now, here in San Diego, I have that power. I have the curse Zianna warned me of, then gave me."

Mickey shrugged. "So, people are disgusting. Now Facebook and Twitter and E-mail and all the other crap gets us to really know our friends, our lovers, our wives and husbands and children. I think you're performing for the cameras with your costumes and tattoos; I think you're poking crap jewelry into your face and your nose in order to punish yourself. You flip the bird to the cameras because you're as lonely and sad and disgusting as the rest of us."

Cassandra smiled. "You're right. If it were just that, I could go on, doing my laundry, going to work, paying my bills, living here in neutral. But something is coming. Something is wrong. I never knew what would happen when I ate the witch's mushroom. What happened was not what I expected. Now I see that something terrible is coming."

Mickey frowned. "What?"

"I'm not sure. It's not only what the cameras tell me, it's what I hear too."

"What do you hear?"

Cassandra had a customer, a young skag-girl who needed a crack pipe. The girl was a devastated thing that hid her pocked face in a hood, and glanced at the world, the cameras. Doom was in her eyes. Cassandra knew from the cameras that this girl sat in the alleys smoking crack and going into unreality. The girl was safe from the cameras; they didn't care that a girl fell through the cracks. The terrible thing that was coming was more important.

"Can you hook me up?" the girl whispered desperately.

"I'm sorry," Cassandra said. "I can sell you a pipe; but no more."

"The cameras are watching us."

"Yes, they are."

The girl left the smoke shop. Mickey tried not to shudder. He did not believe in 2012 predictions. He didn't believe in God or witches or magic or anything supernatural. He considered himself a loser, but a pragmatic one. End of the world shit frankly bored him. This was different.

"You don't even like me, do you?" he asked her.

"I don't know. What difference does it make?"

"To you, maybe nothing."

Cassandra stared out at the boulevard, the people passing by, the skate boarders rolling by in shorts and muscle shirts, the old woman with the wide straw sunhat; the fortiesh guy jogging, stopping to check his wrist, his blood pressure. People desperately afraid of death and their health. People moving in a mechanical way, yet also suspended in a sort of liquid sunshine. She counted those who were talking to themselves.

She knew something was near the day she got home and opened the door of her apartment. She gasped and let out a cry seeing the crone figure sitting on her sofa, like a frightening sculpture of wood.

"Oh, God!" she cried. "Zianna?"

"How do you like your powers, child?" The witch was staring at the painting Cassandra had bought at the flea market: a twisted squirming madness of primary colors. She actually bought it because she read the artist's name and it made her smile: Alexander Nomore.

"He too reads the cameras. Surely you didn't think you were the only one with that power."

"I don't—how did you get here? How did you find out where—"

"It was not easy. But I have ways. How do you like your powers?"

Cassandra tried to shake away the dread: "It wasn't what I expected; it wasn't what I wanted."

"Nothing ever is." The witch stared at the painting. "The mushroom did not give you this curse; it was a common morel I cut up. You were born with this curse. You are not the only one."

"I don't know anything," Cassandra said. "I only feel."

"The age of humans is ending," Zianna said. "We have raced too fast and too reckless. I don't know why I tell you this. I have lived longer than you would believe, child. I have lived in the age of trees and swamps and caves and clay bricks and swords and guns and bombs; of chemicals, of magic; I have even lived in the world just beyond this one, and its delusions of reality."

"What will happen?" Cassandra asked.

"A sickness will happen. The cameras have already seen it, and soon you will see it."

"A sickness?"

"Not one that scientists could recognize. It cannot be cured or treated, because it is not itself a living thing. It has everything to do with the cameras. They see and tell us too much. One learns in the Kentucky hills, if one has the power to see. Humans are pushing too much into their brains, their souls. They are losing privacy;

and they do not see how dangerous it is. A reckoning will begin. You feel it, Cassandra; I know by the way that you live and dress; that you see the future madness. These machines that see us always and hear us always and give us so much . . . they are even now in the trees of Kentucky; they have been watching moonshiners not far from my cabin. But soon, looking down on us, they will give us a strange virus, one that no scientist could have predicted. A virus that has no cure."

"What kind of virus could a computer, or a cell phone or a camera cause?"

"It is a madness virus. Like a computer virus, it only exists in the mind. It feeds on the overload of information. The definition of madness. They see it coming, those who control the cameras. They know that a line has been passed, and they will not be able to stop or control this madness that is coming; that few can see coming."

"How can you know these things? Out there without running water."

"You can call it magic," the witch said. "I do not know how and I do not know why. I suspect that there must be something in fate."

"I see people passing by the shop where I work," Cassandra said. "They're mumbling to themselves, and at first I thought they were talking to handless cell phones. But I'm beginning to see that they aren't wearing cell phones. It's not unusual to see one or two schizophrenics wandering by with their things in a shopping cart. Dirty, worn-down crazy homeless people. But recently there are more. They talk to themselves, and sometimes yell and grip their heads as if voices were tormenting them. A lot of them are clean and dressed in expensive clothes. They don't look homeless, or even poor. Each day their numbers increase."

"It is too late for most people." Ziana shrugged. "Like all pandemics, it will spread everywhere and people will go stupefied mad; but like all pandemics there will be some who will be immune."

"Immune from what?" Cassandra watched the old woman, so out of place with the relentless noise of the city outside the door. How did the witch know anything about the cameras? Or anything about technology?

"Why did you come here?" she asked.

The witch looked sharply at her. "To take you back. Because it is not too late for you. You must go back, Cassandra."

"I can't go back there. I might not be happy anywhere I go; but at least here I'm in my element."

"You are in an element that will change fast. If you do not leave, you will probably not survive what is coming, even though you are immune."

"You came here to take me back. Why?"

"You were not afraid to speak to me, a dirty old woman in a shack. You spoke to me, and you wanted to visit me. You were the daughter I never had."

"And you came out here to San Diego to find me like this?"

"Travel is not yet paralyzed," Zianna said. "It will be soon, so I have to get back to my cabin and my woods."

"You were the only one I missed moving here," Cassandra admitted.

"You do not belong here, child. You wanted to know people, you know people. Now you must get away from the cameras."

"I can't do that. The cameras are everywhere."

"Not everywhere," the witch said. "I am going back to where there are few cameras. When this virus dies out, the cameras will not matter. You must make your own choice."

"I choose to stay here," Cassandra said.

"Knowing the madness that is coming."

"Yes. Because it's always been mad."

"Not like what is coming."

Cassandra smiled at her. "Farewell, Zianna. Maybe we'll meet again."

"Farewell, child. We will never meet again."

She obsessed about it for two full weeks, her mind tearing out terrifying thoughts; her power coming alive. One day something in her mind gave her the answer. It should have not shocked her. Somehow she could sense a disbelief come over the trillion cameras that looked down from almost everywhere.

"See that guy there?"

Mickey looked out the storefront. He was beginning to get spooked. "Another one."

The man on the street would pause in his muttering to tilt his head and pound on his ear, as if to get water out of it.

"Yesterday they fired the 10 o'clock newsman on channel 13. He was beginning to say weird things on the air."

"Yeah, I was watching him. I Do watch the news, when I'm not masturbating."

"I'm sorry I said that to you."

"The guy seemed to be strangely cutting out in the middle of his newscast, like a broken record."

"That's an accurate analogy." Cassandra stared out the storefront. "Something's happening, Mickey; something bad."

He looked at her. "Yeah, 2012. They could have made a better movie."

"No, you don't understand. People are going insane!"

Mickey's Adams apple bobbed. He tried to smile. "That's San Diego."

"Mickey, look out there. It's happening fast—how can it happen so fast?"

"Cass, nothing is happening. We're in a head shop on El Cajon Boulevard. Strange people are going to walk past."

"No. This is different. I think it's going on practically everywhere. Zianna told me to get out of here."

"Yeah, Zianna. She's the witch."

"She told me that she can't die."

"Well, good luck with that one."

Cassandra stared away. "I know you think I'm crazy, I know that. Believe me, I get that everywhere I go. You're going to find out that I'm not. And you're going to find out very soon. Let's have some sarcasm."

Mickey gave her that therapeutic sigh of his that infuriated her. "I don't think you're crazy," he said. "It's just—crazy people walk all over the place. People talking to their cell phones, they look crazy. The guy next door to me talking to his dog, he's crazy."

"This is different."

"I don't see how."

Mickey looked out the storefront and he saw how. Two figures, a man and a woman, but not together, were stumbling out there, hands pressed to their ears. They were babbling. They didn't look like street people; were they drunk?

He turned to Cassandra. "You think this is all because of the cameras? How could cameras do that?"

"No, it's not just the cameras. It's everything. It has invaded us, it is controlling us, and now it is infecting us."

"What is?" Mickey was getting irritated.

"Will you give me your cell phone and let me throw it in the toilet?"

"Uh . . . no."

"Why not?"

"Because, unlike you, I embrace technology. My phone can do everything, and I shamelessly embrace it as my best friend."

"That's it—don't you see? Maybe that's how the virus attacks." She gave him a wicked look. "It's things that don't seem connected. But they are utterly connected. And for some reason they're attacking us. Out of nowhere; and we didn't see it coming and we don't know why it's happening and we don't know how it's happening . . ."

"Like the Black Death."

"Maybe!"

"Oh, come on, Cass. I don't really feel attacked by the cameras—or my cell phone."

"Unless you're immune, you will, Mickey. It's going to happen fast, like a tsunami. It's all built up for this attack."

"How do you know this?"

Cassandra's eyes were dark; she stared out the store window at El Cajon Boulevard. "It's electromagnetic

41

waves or something. It's finally infecting our minds. And now it's speeding up. A virus that isn't organic, and isn't even technically alive. It is something that we've unleashed on ourselves. No one truly knows where a virus comes from, or why it is. Or *what* it is. Only that it has two purposes: to invade and to reproduce. The most fertile ground for this thing is the human mind; that's where it attacks."

"What does this have to do with cameras?"

"The cameras are only the tunnels—the way in. The ways, I should say, because it's coming through cell phones, and computers and many other tunnels. It's growing, and that's why so many people are going crazy."

"Some electromagnetic virus is starting to attack us. Why would it do that?"

"Why do germs attack us? Bacteria. Why would a virus choose to spread and destroy?"

"You tell me why."

"I don't know . . . but maybe it just wants to keep on living."

"You're talking about some super computer virus that—"

"No! I'm talking about a virus like none we ever imagined. Call me insane, Mick, but I've seen what the cameras are seeing, and what they tell each other. It's going to get insane, Mickey; it's going to get real insane."

"How do you know this?"

Cassandra stared out at the street. A man was walking past, carrying a camera, one of the digital ones they planted on roofs and under eaves. He was muttering to himself; suddenly he stopped and stared into the shop at her. His eyes were dazed at first, but then they focused down to weapons. His mouth slowly chewed on some words that she couldn't understand. She shuddered, looked down and closed her eyes tight. When she looked up, he was gone.

"That's a question that I can't answer," she said. "Not yet."

She thought about running. As the city quickly began spinning into chaos, she wondered if she should have followed Zianna back. But she had no money, no car. Few groceries, no survival equipment. She was as ill-prepared as she could be when it hit. There was a knock on her door at seven a.m., and it was a shell-shocked Mickey. He brushed past her, quickly shut her front door and locked it. He managed to prop his skateboard against the wall. He was pale and shaking.

"What is this?" She tried to control her voice.

He couldn't speak for a few seconds. He seemed to try and get himself together.

"Mickey, what's wrong? I don't want to be late for work. You're supposed to be there already."

"There's no work, Cass." He glanced at the locked door. "Not anymore."

"What are you talking about?"

"You know what the hell I'm talking about! You told me it would happen."

Now she could smell the smoke, and she glanced into the kitchen to see if it was the oven or something. She felt vaguely embarrassed; No one had ever been inside her apartment. Now Mickey stood there looking at the air mattress that was her dismal bed.

"What's that smoke?"

"Fires. Damn near everything out there is on fire! Don't you know?"

Cassandra had sipped too much wine last night.

She read the camera outside the security gate of her complex. It was aimed at the northwest, where great clouds of smoke rose above El Cajon Boulevard. She saw cars and SUVs piled up on the curbs and intersections. She saw others careening out of control, as if two blocks away was a slow motion NASCAR pileup. She saw smoke sweeping across her neighborhood, borne on the Pacific breeze. She saw neighbors rushing out, some trying to read their cell phones, some pounding their heads at a madness that was hitting them like a heart attack.

Mickey folded himself up on her small couch and cradled his head in his hands. "Is this thing going to get us, Cass?"

"I—don't know. Zianna warned me that I might not survive it."

"I can't believe this is happening. I can't believe this."

Cassandra unlocked and opened the door to her street-level apartment. She looked out at a strange quiet madness. People wandered like zombies, some of them pounding their heads. Cars rolled slowly out of control, crunching into other cars. It was a scene of madness, but lazy madness, the world going insane in slow motion. A scene from some television mini-series.

"Cass, please shut the door," Mickey said. "Please shut the door."

But she couldn't. She stared out at a world she had seen coming but never really believed. Even now, looking out at the sudden infection of it all, she questioned her sanity. She saw a neighbor on his deck, studying the madness. The ex-professor now alcoholic who always walked his dog at night in a stumbling stupor. He didn't look insane. It wasn't infecting everybody, not yet. She didn't feel insane; Mickey didn't seem to be insane.

Yet.

She turned and stared at Mickey. He was scared shitless, but he wasn't a zombie, not like some of the people out there. She looked out her door and saw the stylish jogging lady with the cats, who was always stuck onto her cell phone, even as she went out shopping. The woman wandered lost toward El Cajon Boulevard, tripping on her high heels, talking weirdly to no one.

"Is that going to happen to us?" Mickey gave her a white stare.

"I don't know. It hasn't yet." Cassandra studied the world, the crippled world that was dying in disbelief. Maybe you always die in disbelief. She stared at the smoke growing bigger and darker over El Cajon Boulevard. Why were they starting fires? What did that mean?

She remembered when her mother fell before her from a massive heart attack. How her mother kept gasping, even after her heart had stopped beating. The look on her face—disbelief.

"Cass, can you close the door—please?"

She closed and locked the door. Mickey was puffing hard, trying to cope. Cassandra surprised herself by being glad that he was here, in her grim apartment. She knew him, as she knew everybody, by reading the cameras. He was scared and bewildered, and she was too. But he wasn't infected—yet. She read the camera outside, seeing a zomboid world, things crumbling in an unreal way.

"It's the cell phones!" Mickey cried out. "It's not the cameras."

"It's both," she said. "It's all."

"I can't believe this," he said. "I—just can't believe this is happening."

Cassandra blinked her eyes at the apartment camera, but it suddenly went dead. She could hear sounds of fear beyond the door of her apartment. Moans of despair and madness, and most of all,disbelief.

"I wonder if I made it go off," she said.

"What?"

"That camera. The one on the guard gate. I tried to look at it and it went out."

"Cass, tell me what this is!"

"I don't know what it is, Mickey! I think it's everything coming together in some sort of vanishing point. Electro-magnetic germs submerging us, and then infecting us."

"Electro-magnetic germs." Mickey jumped at a scream that echoed outside of the door. "Where the hell are the sirens!"

"What?"

"The police, paramedics, firemen. I hear that crazy shit out there. I don't hear any sirens. There are no sirens, Cass!"

"I'm trying to read the cameras on El Cajon—Jesus, I'm shutting them off!"

"Shutting off the cameras?"

"They're going black. Shut off your cell phone, Mickey."

"What?"

"Shut the damn thing off! Now!"

Mickey fumbled his 300 dollar i-phone out. He shut it off, and Cassandra felt a weird and fatal calmness. She had always believed humans were doomed to extinction. Somehow she had always known it would happen. But not so fast, not like this.

"I don't have much food here," she said to him. "Some fruit cocktail; some carrots and canned tuna."

"I'm not hungry," Mickey said. He listened to what was going on out there.

"This is—so crazy. This—what the hell is happening?"

"Zianna said it would come as a virus. I think it's an electric virus that sat in silence until we welcomed it in. The electro-magnetics that we've come to love and depend upon, they're attacking us. It's the perfect virus."

"Jesus, Cass. This can't be true."

"That's what they said in the ancient days: When the bubonic plague hit Europe. People wandered like living skeletons. They asked God how this could happen, how death could swarm over people like that."

"Cass—don't talk like that. It's freaking me out."

"It might be what it is, Bobby." She listened to the screams and noises coming from beyond her apartment door. She heard no sirens. Mickey had sensed the fear of all: There was smoke and flame and carnage and car wrecks and madness out there; but there were no sirens.

"What do you think we should do?" he asked.

"I don't know. Wait this thing out?"

"I should get back to my apartment."

"Mickey, are you crazy?"

"Not yet. But what if that changes, Cass?"

She rushed to open the apartment door again. "Neither one of us is crazy. It's not infecting everybody."

In fact, most of the people gathered outside, although utterly stunned, didn't have the infection—yet. They all chattered fearfully, but it was different; they were chattering at one another, not themselves. She stepped outside and traded nervous looks with her neighbors. Red fire glowed all along the distance; it seemed all of El Cajon Boulevard was on fire. She read the near cameras. They were black spots in her eyes.

But a dying audio echoed dead in her ears, and then went silent: *Get away get away get away . . .*

She stared at a chaos that was growing beyond the flames and car wrecks. She heard her neighbors all shriek as a helicopter plunged down near Lake Murray and sent a great explosion into the night.

"God!" she said. "Oh God!"

"Holy—did you see that?"

"I've got to get away," she said. "The witch was right—if I don't get away, I'm going to die."

"Get away? Where?"

Cassandra rushed into her apartment and began gathering up absolute essentials. "How much food do you have in your place, Mick?"

"I don't know, some frozen dinners."

"Okay. I'm going to bag what I can, and I'm going to head east."

"East—what are you talking about?"

"You can come with me if you want. But I warn you, we'll be hoofing it. And hopefully we'll get out of here before a million people are going to be hoofing it."

"You're talking about walking out of here east? Do you know what—"

"Come with me or not," she said.

"Okay, okay; don't freak out," Mickey said. "I might be able to get a car from my brother's lot—a loaner. We can drive east and see how bad this is."

"Let's walk two blocks up there to El Cajon and see."

They walked up to El Cajon Boulevard. People were everywhere, standing staring at the smoke. Some of them were insane from the cameras—all of them were growing insane with fear. Dogs barked and howled, voices strained the air:

"A plane crashed. Maybe a Navy jet."

"A terrorist attack."

"I didn't feel no earthquake."

"Why's everything so crazy? What the hell is happening?"

Both directions on El Cajon were littered with wrecked cars, some of them on fire. Buildings were on fire as far as the eyes. The head shop was a blown out black shell. Amid the wreckage, the infected walked as if they were in a crazy trance, oblivious to what was going on. That was the scariest image she remembered.

"We couldn't even make it to your brother's lot," she said. "And we couldn't drive a block after that. I have to get moving east, on foot. You can come with me; but I'm moving now."

Mickey stared toward downtown San Diego. He could see nothing through the clouds of smoke. The entire city was on fire.

"I've got some cash at my place."

"No!" she said. "We'll die if we try to get to your place. In less than a month, cash isn't going to mean anything. Mick, we're in the middle of the modern

Black Death. People are going to be clogging every road, path and highway trying to get out of here. The ones who aren't yet infected are going to get desperately away."

Cassandra stared at San Diego, enveloped in flame and smoke. The sight made her think she was dreaming. Or in some kind of horror movie. She thought of the witch, Zianna.

"We start heading west," Mickey said. He could barely control his voice.

"West is the Pacific Ocean. I'm going east. Come with me or not, that's what I'm going to do."

"I meant east. Jesus! Cass . . . if we stay still, hold up, last this thing out . . ."

"Then we'll die," she said.

"Okay, okay . . . God!" Mickey stared out at the burning madness that was San Diego. Was this happening in Boston, where his folks lived? Or Omaha, where his sister lived?

"This is a nuclear bomb," he said. "A terrorist—"

"No! Come on, Mick. We both have to toughen up, or we're going to die."

"This isn't happening," he said. "Cass, this can't be happening."

She dragged him back to her apartment. She hefted the backpack she had packed. She thought of the witch who claimed to have lived forever. The witch she had met at a grey cedar cabin in the wrinkled Kentucky woods.

She thought about leaving Mickey behind; he wasn't infected, but he wasn't even prepared for this.

But I'm not either, she thought. If this is the end of everything, at least he's company.

"Everybody you see around you—if they're not infected—everybody around us will have to get out of here, one way or another. They're not going to drive out and they're not going to skateboard out. I read the cameras, and they told me about this. There are, in America, a trillion cameras. That gave us a virus of the mind. If you want to try to go on living, then come with me. But this might come down to caveman shit. The world is burning to death, Mickey."

"How can you know this?"

She hefted the backpack and started walking east, on a parallel path to El Cajon Boulevard. She knew that east were the mountains. She had thought about going south into Mexico, in case the madness had not struck so hard there. North was Los Angeles, where the cameras had told her it was far worse. Like the witch said, Cassandra could see what this was; she could see how it came and what it would do. Cameras blinked off as she and Mickey walked east, slowly out of burning San Diego.

"I'm turning off the cameras," she said. "Every block we walk, I'm turning off cameras."

Mickey coughed at the smoke that was blowing from the ocean. "Is that going to help us?"

"Nothing is going to help us but us."

"How are you doing that? Shutting off the cameras?"

"I don't know."

"Okay. Do we have like a plan?"

"We make it to Alpine."

Hand in hand they went east, trying not to see the madness exploding around them. People everywhere, screaming, waving their arms, some walking mad, as if nothing was happening. Baltimore Street was a mess of car wrecks, cars smashed against trees, cars smoking and twisted all over. Cars burning like bonfires. They went into the canyon and climbed out. They rested in a Wendy's parking lot and looked west at the impossible fire. People ran everywhere. San Diego was being destroyed. Fire and smoke dominated the skies. And there were no sirens, no signs that anyone was coming.

People ran up to them: "What is this! What is this!"

"This is too freaky," Mickey said. His face was pasty grey.

Cassandra pushed away a woman who was screaming into her face. She felt the blistering heat blowing their way from burning San Diego.

"This is going to be bad, Mick. This is getting real bad."

Mickey surprised her by getting control of himself: "I know that. I'm not stupid. We have to try and get as far east of here as we can get. That means climbing mountains and not having any fucking money. But all we have to worry about now is getting the hell out of here. I get it."

She looked at him. She heard the explosions in the distance, she didn't know from where. Infected people moved below, in the valley. She could see all of them talking to themselves. She looked east away at the mountains, and Alpine. She looked west at the bonfire that was San Diego.

"We move east as fast as we can," She said. "No matter what, we have to get out of here!"

Mickey gave her a scared smile. "So let's go."

Denton, Ne ...

This is a true story. I don't write many of them, but this one is true, and it happened one day.

As I mentioned previously, I work at the store in Denton, Nebraska, a small community about a dozen miles southwest of the city of Lincoln, which is—but screw that, you don't care about Nebraska. I don't much either, and I live here.

There's something about this store in Denton, Nebraska. It's old and beat up and the floor is ugly. Nothing like one of the sparkling convenience stores you'll find on 27th Street or 56th Street in Lincoln, with the car wash and all that.

Here you look out and you see the little red-haired girl with freckles who always rides her bike around Denton, and sometimes parks it at the town playground, a rubber-turfed aluminum and plastic red green blue yellow contortion of slides and ladders and bridges and tunnels.

Always she comes into the store to buy Sweet Tarts, and always we talk. Today I asked her how school was going.

"It's okay," she said. "But a new boy moved in down the street."

"Where?"

"Right over there." She pointed west, three houses down. "He was at the park today, and he was being mean to everybody."

"What did he do?"

"He told me he was going to beat me up. And I told him he'd better leave me alone or I'd beat Him up."

"I'll bet you would." I smiled. "It might be that he likes you, but doesn't know how to say it. Boys are stupid like that."

"Well, I'm not scared of him. I'll fight him if he keeps up."

She took her candy out of the store, got on her bicycle and rode defiantly down the block. I traded laughs with Gil Snell, the next customer. I rang up his 16 pack Busch Lite, some beef jerky and a carton of Marlborough Reds. Shannon came into the store, and behind her Myron. Shannon was a 20 year old sweetheart, born and raised in Denton, Nebraska. She was crying.

Gil left the store, but returned moments later, reading his receipt.

Oh crap, I thought.

"What's wrong, Gil?"

"Well, I got out to the truck and I read my receipt. I don't think you charged me enough for what I bought."

I read the receipt. He was right, in both senses of the word.

"I don't want you to get into any trouble," he said.

When Gil left, Shannon bought a Coke and a candy bar. I asked her why she was crying.

"My boyfriend broke up with me."

"What did he do?"

"He's been seeing some—other girl. He doesn't want me anymore."

I smiled at her. "Shannon, I've been around the block a few times. And there's only one thing I can tell you that I know is true, and I don't want you ever to forget it."

She blew her nose on a napkin. All her scratch tickets came up losers.

"What?" she asked me.

"Shannon, I don't know your boyfriend. I only know one thing: if he lets you slip away, he's friggin crazy."

"That's right," Myron said behind her. Myron was a retired post officer, sixty-five years old. He liked to haunt Denton in sweat pants and slippers; but when the weather was bad, he drove the rattle-trap ugliest 5-toned pickup truck on Earth up and down the street. Everybody knew him and everybody loved him. Nobody knew where he was going.

"If he cheated on you," Myron said. "Then he ain't worth it."

Shannon smiled behind her. "Hi, Myron."

"The guy's crazy," I said.

Shannon took her candy bar and Coke and left the store.

"How's it going, Myron?"

"Ahhh, not so good. Give me a small bottle of vodka and a pack of Marlborough Lites. No, make it full flavor, in the box. What the hell."

"What's the matter?"

"Oh, I just got back from the doctor. I've got cancer."

"My God. Cancer."

"Yeah, and what pisses me off is it's in my ass. Prostrate cancer. Jesus, if you have to get cancer, why does it have to be in your ass? That's pretty damn humiliating."

"What's the prognosis, Myron?"

"It ain't good. I won't be around for long."

"I can't imagine that."

He laughed. "Well, if you can imagine cancer of the ass, then you should be able to imagine anything."

"What are you going to do?"

"Oh, I'm going to go home, get a little drunk on the couch, smoke a few cigarettes and watch some television. You have a good day, Jim."

"You too, Myron."

I watched Myron drive away in his outrageously ugly pickup truck. I had listened to local guys debating whether it was a Ford or a Chevy or a Dodge, and what year it could be. Maybe it was all three and had no year.

I stared out of the convenience store at Denton. The mud-colored clouds had finally burned away, and pure sun lighted the town. Down the block the Daily Double, a cowboy keno bar and restaurant, was doing sluggish business. It was Saturday, the kids were out of school, and I could hear them yelling and playing at the town park just across the street.

Less than 200 folks live here. Count the local farm families and that's about 250 or so . . .

The world is full of evil and misery. The world is full of people who will rip you off if they can. The world is full of terrible weakness—cowardice, selfishness. There are places of lush beauty, tropical seductions, traps. There are many places on Earth that would make you sick that they could be so evil. So many places that make you despair.

This is not one of those places.

Morning Of Blood . . .

Getting drunk until you pass out—excuse me, "Black out"—is not wise. It happened to me a few times, and I will advise the reader against it. One whiskey leads to relaxation, another to blinking hilarity, then . . . well, next morning you wake up sick and ashamed and dreading what idiotic thing you might have pulled beyond your memory.

I've lost more than a few girlfriends this way, and it's a miracle the police never pulled me over and shoved my stupid face into rock bottom. I've come awake too many times to shame—but this was the first time it went beyond that into pure horror.

This was not waking up to a bed soaked in urine and a floor slick with forgotten vomit. This time I woke up to the coppery smell of blood and a strange person butchered and bloody on my apartment floor.

My pasted eyes sprang open, and then stared down at the sight, and my brain wanted to scutter back into sleep. But you don't go back to sleep after seeing that. Hangovers should be brutal lessons, but not this: a guy sprawled on the floor in a shallow blood-pool—and now I felt the knife on my pillow, stained with blood.

Oh God, Oh God!

I couldn't have done this, because even drunk I'm less violent than a rabbit.

I stared down at the bloody victim, a large man with tattoos and muscles. I squeezed shut my eyes and took long, wheezy breaths. How many whiskies? My thoughts went crazy. Oh, God, Please. This must be some booze nightmare, some hallucination.

My eyes crawled open: "Ahhh!"

There was the corpse, bloody on the floor. I stared down at it, sickened beyond any hangover.

"Oh, Please—No!" I heard my voice, clogged with old cigarette smoke.

I swiped the bloody knife from the bed, and it thumped onto the carpet. I stared down at it. I didn't own a knife like that. I stared at the bloody corpse on the floor. How could a skinny me stab to death what appeared to be a massive biker? Even drunk I could never overcome a guy with those muscles and tattoos.

"This can't be," I said. "It just can't be!"

As I stared down at the corpse, it suddenly winked at me. I scrambled back in terror.

"Oh, God!"

The corpse smiled at me. He rose up from the carpet, his muscled arms doing a kind of push-up.

"Ahhh! God!!!"

"Whoa, calm down, Dude," the corpse said to me. "Don't worry, this stuff washes out pretty easy."

"What?"

"This fake blood."

My gritty eyes stared down at the knife. "I—don't—understand . . ."

"Calm down. You didn't murder anybody."

"Oh, God—I feel sick."

"Yeah, we get that a lot." The man smiled at me, then sat calmly down on my writing chair. "I apologize for freaking you out. But that's our business."

"Your what?"

"Intense Interventions. That's the name of our company. Now take some deep breaths, Dude, and relax. You're blessed with friends who care about you."

"Relax! What?"

The man was covered in blood. Yet he had a comforting smile for me. "Sorry for waking you up like this. It's our business."

"You're a zombie!"

"No. Just an actor doing a gig. Calm down, Dude."

"Too many whiskies," I heard my voice whisper, staring down at my blood-smeared bed. "Too many whiskies."

"That's right. You have a drinking problem, and sometimes alcoholics need to be shocked into sobriety. That's what my company does."

"Your—company."

"Right. Intense Interventions. We take cases that require more than counseling."

I glared at him. "Who paid you to do this?"

"People who care about you."

"Who?"

"That's not important. Did I scare you?"

"Jesus God—Yes!"

"Good. That's my job. And don't worry; this red dye washes out with ordinary soap and water."

I stared down at the knife on the floor. "Intense Interventions?"

"We hope to make a difference."

"I'm going to be sick."

"Good. That's really our goal. And after you're sick—what then? Are you going to need a drink?"

My eyelids tried to stick together as I blinked them. The knife lay glittering on the carpet.

"It's your job to horrify people?"

"Yes, pretty much."

"I see . . ."

I stared at the blood-stained man. I stared down at the knife, the bloody carpet.

"I see."

Rex . . .

When I died I didn't know what to expect . . . a tunnel, a light? Golden arches—or nothing.

Probably the last thing I expected was a green prairie, a wood fence, a flagstone path and a talking beagle.

"You look kind of confused," the dog said to me. "That's okay; just follow me."

This was a crazy dream, of course, but I followed the beagle down the flagstone path that seemed to lead forever into a prairie distance.

"I'm Rex," the dog said. "I'll be your guide."

"Rex?" I kind of chuckled. This was a dream, Wizard of Ozish—enjoy . . . however, I did have the vague memory of a heart attack. "Rex?" I said.

"That's my name. Do you have a problem with that?"

"No, it's just that—"

"It means King. It's Latin."

"I know it is."

"Well, you're now dead. This is what is beyond life."

"A talking dog."

"Do you have a problem with dogs?"

"No. But this can't be. I mean . . ."

"I get that a lot."

"All right. Now I'm scared. I'm really scared. I remember thinking 'I'm having a heart attack!' I remember that. But I thought I was dreaming."

"You always think you're dreaming."

"Okay . . . look, Rex, I'm getting really scared."

"What are you scared of?"

"You're a talking dog! You're a dog who's talking to me and leading me—I don't know where. This has to be a dream. But it doesn't feel like a dream."

"This isn't a dream. You really are dead, and my advice is: relax and enjoy it."

"Enjoy being dead."

"Look at it this way: you'll never have to go to the bathroom anymore." The beagle barked out a laugh. "That one never gets old."

"A talking dog . . . this can't be."

"Oh, shut up and enjoy the day."

"I'm scared. I'm really scared."

"What the hell are you scared of!"

"If I'm truly dead . . . I'm scared of God."

The beagle padded up the cobbled path, saying nothing. The path followed a raw fence into green, windblown prairie. The sun fell warm over this unreal world. A dream . . . it had to be a dream. But it didn't feel like it.

"I can live a better life. I'm ashamed of some of the things I do."

"Did," Rex said. "You're dead, remember? It's too late for regrets, so don't worry about it."

"Am I?" I looked down at the talking beagle. I looked down the flagstone path. "I mean, I'm talking to a talking dog. We're walking down this path that doesn't seem to have an end . . ."

"You're dead, and this is what's beyond. You want to stop and rest awhile?"

"No, unless you're tired."

"I don't get tired," Rex said.

"It's just that—" I made a nervous laugh. "This isn't what it's supposed to be. This scenery, the fence, this path that doesn't seem to have an end." I looked down at Rex: "You're a beagle, aren't you?"

"That's what they tell me."

"Purebred?"

He looked at me. "What?"

"Are you a purebred beagle?"

"They say I am. But you never know. I drool a lot, so there might have been a bulldog in the wood shed." Rex barked out a laugh that scared me. "What difference does it make?"

"Well, it doesn't. I only know that I'm not dead, and that this is a dream."

"How do you know that, Dick?"

"My name's Dave! You can't even get my name right. I'm not dead, and you're not a talking dog. My name is Dave, not Dick! When you die, you don't find yourself walking down a flagstone path with a talking dog—who doesn't even know your name!"

"You have a problem with dogs, don't you, Dick?"

"No! I don't have a problem with dogs. It's just that—I'm scared. I'm scared of God. And my name is Dave."

"I know; I'm just pulling your chain. Inside joke. Okay, Dave, you're now dead. Stop worrying. You spent your whole damn life worrying. Now, why can't you relax and enjoy this day? It's a beautiful day, why not enjoy it? Smell the wind."

It was a sweet wind, lonely and lovely. "It's beautiful," I said. "That wind."

"I can smell it a hundred times better than you." The beagle looked at me. "Why do you look so sad when your eyes go up that path?"

"I'm not sure. Are we going to Heaven? Is that where this path leads?"

"You ask too many questions," Rex said. "Why?"

"Why? Why do you think! It's just that—I worry about my judgment. I'm afraid that I am dead, I'm afraid of God, that He's going to . . ."

"Judge you? Then maybe punish you?"

"Yes!"

"He doesn't go that way. God is angry and vengeful? That's B.S. You wouldn't believe the slack He cuts."

"I never believed. I never went to church. I never prayed, I never believed in God. I thought when I died that was it, there was never anything beyond. I was never born again. I never believed! I never believed there was anything beyond."

"That's the point, Dave," Rex said. "You don't know, nobody knows. That's the fun of it."

"The fun of it?"

"Yes! When you were alive did you hate people?"

"Well . . . no, I didn't really hate anybody."

"Did you hurt anybody? I mean like really bad."

"No, I don't think so."

"I know you didn't. I've got your whole life down. Anyway, I know you didn't murder anybody."

"No."

"Remember the girl who came up to your farmhouse after she'd wrecked her car?"

My stomach jumped. "How do you know about that?"

"She was traumatized, she was scared and helpless and damn near out of her mind."

"She wrecked her dad's car."

"The girl came running up to your farmhouse. She was scared to death. You remember."

"She was scared to call her dad and tell him."

"You could have taken advantage of her, Dave. And she was as vulnerable as a teen age girl could be."

"What?"

"You could have raped her and you probably would have gotten away with it. Just you and this terrified young girl at your isolated farmhouse."

"Raped her? What are you talking about?"

"I'm talking about the only thing that matters. You did everything you could to calm her down and protect her. You called her dad, you walked down to the highway with her to wait for him, you talked to her dad and asked him to go easy on her, she was pretty upset. Then you drove your tractor down there and tugged the car out of the ditch, and when the girl's dad asked you what you wanted in pay, what did you say to him, Dave?"

"I don't remember."

"You said three little words: pass it on. That's what God cares about. And he did pass it on. And it got passed on."

"How do you know these things?"

"You ask too many questions." The beagle padded up the flagstone path. "You didn't even think about being evil, did you?"

"No, I didn't."

"You never believed, you never prayed, you never joined a religion. You think God cares about that? He doesn't care what you believe, or if you don't believe. He cares about what you did. If you lived a good life, that's all God cares about. He wasn't all that pleased when you punched out Jeff Sherman in the fourth grade . . . but the guy had it coming."

"My god, I'd forgotten that. How do you know these things?"

"God was pissed that you did it to impress a girl. Audrey Cress. Remember her?"

"Yes, I remember her."

"Where is she now, and what is she doing?"

"I don't know."

"There you go."

I stared up the flagstone path. "What are Heaven and Hell like?"

"Heaven is a lot of work. You don't sit on your dead ass in Heaven—unless you're a writer."

"What about Hell?"

"Hell is nothing, and you kind of wanted that, didn't you?"

"Well . . ."

"You did—admit it!"

"Yes. Not having any more worries. No pain, no sadness. No struggles."

"Well, sorry, but that's Hell. Hell is the end of everything; Heaven is the beginning of everything. And they don't like folks sitting around on their dead asses."

I looked down at Rex, a beagle who seemed far wiser than me.

"It's weird," I said. "But I'm kind of hoping that I Am dead, and not just dreaming."

"Trust me, you're dead. So relax; enjoy the day, enjoy the wind."

We walked over the green hill, the wind ruffling grass far over the horizon. I reached over and touched the rough fence. I thought absurdly that it was made of hickory. Rex padded calmly over the flagstones, his nose taking in that sweet wind.

"I thought the path to Heaven was gold," I tried a joke. "Not common flagstone."

"Gold's too expensive." Rex barked out a laugh. "You did okay, Dave. You weren't Saint Peter, but you did okay. Now's the time to relax."

"Okay. But . . . a talking dog?"

Rex paused and gave me a narrow look. "You have some problem with dogs."

"No. It's just . . . I don't know. How can I know?"

The beagle smiled at me, if a dog can smile. "Don't you know, Dave?"

"I don't! I'm nervous about all this . . . you know, sins I might have committed."

"I get that a lot."

"What about you, Rex; did you commit sins?"

"Like hunting foxes, that kind of thing?"

"Yes."

"I did okay. I was no Saint Bernard, but I did okay." The beagle gave me a sidelong glance. "That was a joke. You could at least pretend to laugh."

"If this truly is the road to God . . . I'm scared."

"What's He going to do, kill you? You're already dead."

"Are you God?"

"Am I—do I look like God?"

"I don't know. I'm sure God can change forms, that kind of thing—take on disguises."

"You worry too much and you asked too many questions. And like most folks, you can't enjoy what you have when you have it."

"Did you ever fall in love?"

(My God, I'm asking this of a talking dog. This is a dream, or I'm insane, or I'm dead. I didn't know which I wished for).

"I fell in love once, with a poodle, go ahead and laugh. She was a looker, but pretty high maintenance, if you know what I mean. Fifty dollar haircuts? I never got a haircut in my life."

I had to laugh. I gazed out at the green waves of prairie. I felt the warm sun, I smelled the sweet wind. "This is pretty," I said.

"Were you ever in love, Dave?"

"I think you already know the answer to that."

"You're picking it up. Good for you."

I had to laugh; it wasn't something I could control.

"What's so funny all at once?" the dog asked me.

"I don't know. The thought of you and a poodle. I'm sorry!"

"You can't laugh at my jokes, but you Can laugh at the heartache of my life. Thanks, Dave."

"This is just so crazy. You have to forgive me. But, Rex—what color was she?"

"Huh?"

"No, but first: what was her name? What was the poodle's name?"

"Her name was Misty."

"Okay, what color was Misty?"

"You don't even want to know."

"I do. I do, Rex."

"She was pink. Okay, laugh your ass off. She'd been dyed pink. Go ahead, laugh."

I did laugh. I took in the warm sunshine, the smell of fresh grass.

"There's nothing to worry about anymore," Rex said.

"I know that now."

The Day I Got Drunk
And Decapitated A Squirrel . . .

Let's be clear: I didn't mean to do it. I'm not going to blame the Bacardi. True, if it were not for the rum the unfortunate thing could never have happened; but I take full responsibility.

Just know: the squirrel was an asshole, a true pest by definition. It stored acorns in my attic, and when it skittered across the attic floor it often made me jump up from a stupor, believing witches were scratching to get in. I'm not a full believer in the supernatural. But the squirrel possessed a crazy crackhead energy, and never seemed to sleep, so I wondered about him. And you don't need witches in the house.

But I digress. I don't dislike squirrels. I love watching them scamper about the giant old maples that hang green and shady along the street. There is something very soothing and delightful watching squirrels in the trees.

IN THE TREES; but this jerk wanted my attic, probably knowing that I would be too afraid to climb up into that creepy place that stunk of dust, where a sinister bare bulb dangled down from the shadows. If I crept up to the attic to see, would the squirrel be there—violently startled by my invasion—and would it attack me?

I rent on Jones Street (I know, that says it all), in an old two story with a storage attic. The squirrel had homesteaded this attic over a month ago, and finally I feared that it would drive me mad. It had to be chased away. Next door, just beyond a plum bush, lived old Mrs. Crabtree, who advised me to simply climb up to the roof and staple wire mesh wherever it could get in.

"Otherwise," she said. "Squirrels won't be chased away. You're better off killing them."

"I don't really want to kill it."

"Well, then climb up there and shut off his entry."

"It's a long way up there," I said doubtfully. "I don't have a ladder."

"Old Zimmerman down at the hardware store'll sell you one. They come in handy."

"Yeah . . . . and to be carrying wire mesh and a staple gun . . ."

She looked at me as if I was a pussy—which is true. But even if I could climb up there to foil the squirrel's plans, what if it was in the attic and I wound up stapling it INSIDE? Or if in panic it attacked my face—two stories up on a ladder . . . no, that wasn't the best plan. It might have been Mrs. Crabtree wanting to rid the neighborhood of another alcoholic.

"So, Mrs. Crabtree; if the squirrel was in your attic, what would you do?"

(I was pretty sure that at age 89 she wouldn't climb a ladder up there).

"I'd kill him," she said. "There are poisons for that kind of thing."

"Squirrel poison?"

"Of course. Old Man Zimmerman down at the hardware store'll sell you some. People like squirrels, I know; but they cause more damage than you think. And if one was in my attic—why . . ."

"You'd kill it."

Studying the trees, I was shocked to see the criminal itself, cheeks bloated with acorns, scampering along a branch that loomed directly over my roof.

"You should go up there and trim that tree branch back," Mrs. Crabtree advised. "Though the squirrel jumps farther than you think."

We stood on the sidewalk and watched the squirrel dance merrily up my roof and disappear into the attic.

"There's your entryway," she said. "Trim back that branch, or even if you kill this one, others will follow."

"Hmmm."

Yeah, climb up there bearing a chainsaw. Terrible plan C. I would hire a professional to do it, but I don't have that kind of money. An outlaw squirrel shouldn't be able to bring about danger, torment and huge expenses.

"Squirrel poison," I murmered.

The crone tapped her walnut cane on the sidewalk. "It's the easiest way."

Except that I would have to climb up to that attic and behold what was up there. Fewer places are creepier than attics, but it was the only way to get poison up there. Then, of course I'd have to venture back up there to retrieve its corpse, which would be contorted forever in agony. Hmmmm.

"What if it's building a nest up there?" I asked. "What if it has babies?"

"Pups," Mrs. Crabtree said. "They're called pups. And it's a male, so don't worry."

"How can you tell it's a male?"

"I just can. You'll see."

"All right. Much as I don't want to, I suppose I'll try the squirrel poison."

"Go down to the hardware store and talk to Old Man Zimmerman."

Old Man Zimmerman was in his mid-seventies, and had probably been born hating everybody. I came into his store only occasionally, but I knew he didn't like me. Behind the counter, he squinted at me over the top of his glasses as I explained the situation.

"First off, I don't sell squirrel poison here," he said. "Second, Old Lady Crabtree lied telling you that's the only way to kill a squirrel. It ain't even the best way. You can kill one with rat poison, I suppose; that ain't what I'd do."

"I'd rather scare it away. I don't really want to kill it."

"You Do want to kill it. It's the only way."

"All right."

"The squirrel, you know, is first cousin to a rat."

"I didn't know that." I gave him the deferential look you give people who don't like you. I didn't want to kill the squirrel; but what else could be done?

"So what's the best way to make it go away—to kill it?"

"How do you get rid of a rat?" he demanded.

"Well, I suppose—a rat trap?"

"There you go. Let me show you something."

I followed Zimmerman down an aisle of sundry hardware goods. We came to a grim section that seemed to advertise a lot of things with skulls and bones on them. Then he handed me a monstrous device, three times the size of a mouse trap, its thick steel mechanism glinting under the lights.

"Good God," I said.

"Just a rat trap, don't go soft. But these are top of the line, and the most powerful brand. You set it with peanut butter."

I knew how to set a mouse trap, of course. The principle was the same with a rat trap; but this thing looked like it could take off your hand.

"This will kill the thing, eh?"

"What do you think?" He drew back the death spring and let the trapeze go with a loud gunshot that made me jump. Old Man Zimmerman chuckled. He was an obnoxious man, who didn't care for fools, and the look he was giving me suggested both.

I bought the awful thing, and smeared it with peanut butter; but I had to drink three rum and cokes before I could screw up the courage to venture with it up to the attic. Ghosting open the trapdoor to the attic, I shone my flashlight around. A cobwebby place, so dusty that everything looked grey. I saw the stash of acorns in a corner and the triangle of sunlight that marked the rodent's doorway. Crawling into the odious place, I set the rat trap, danced away from it, and counted my fingers.

That wasn't so bad. Now all I had to do was wait for the SNAP! And crawl back up there with a heavy duty trash bag—if it truly killed him and didn't just piss him off. I looked at the wicked thing sitting there; the squirrel would have to be pretty stupid to even approach it.

And he was. Only two rum-and-cokes later I jumped up from the couch at the SNAP! from above—then silence.

I didn't want to go back up there. I was too drunk to try and get up there to see—so that was exactly what I did, proud of my guts and determination. I was gloved, and I remembered a large trash bag. I again opened up the trapdoor and shone the flashlight. What I saw sickened and terrified me.

I don't know any of you well enough to know if you've ever come across a squirrel dead by rat trap. I'm sure many of you have squashed them with your cars. It was not that I had followed advice and killed the squirrel; but the trap had chopped its head off and tossed it a good six inches from the body. The severed squirrel head looked at me in dead astonishment, and I felt a strange Edgar Alan Poe moment.

Well, it had invaded my turf; and I was rid of the skittering racket from above; and I didn't see a nest of newborns; and it was stupid to mess with such an obvious death trap, so in the home owner's sense of things, he had it coming. I held my lunch and managed to get the head and its former body into the trash bag. He may indeed have been infected with rabies or something. He shouldn't have looked at me with those huge brown eyes, as if— sharing a house— we had been pals.

I managed to make it back down to the couch and here was R and C number six. Still, the eyes of the decapitated squirrel haunted me and made me oozie in the stomach. Staring into the eyes of a dead squirrel, that wouldn't have upset me so much. It was the lonely and disconnected head with those big eyes that got to me.

This being a morality tale warning the reader against alcohol and animal abuse, I must conclude that its reader should not do what I did, for it will haunt me all my life.

Only one good thing came from the awful event: I no longer have nightmares about witches.

The Getaway . . .

"I've got to get out of these clothes—fast."

"What are you talking about!" Lindsey blinked her eyes furiously. "We don't have a change of clothes!"

"They'll spot me, sure as hell."

I glanced around the brick alley wing at the sun-bright city, the people and cars moving in quiet roar and energy. Succulent restaurant odors swam with the taxi fumes.

"Do you see them?"

"I don't know. I don't know."

I wished Lindsey would quit blinking her eyes like that. I was scared enough.

"What do you mean, you don't know?"

I slid back away from the mouth of the alley. Brick-smell, carbon, was on my hands. "Lindsey, please be quiet . . . I have to think. I didn't spot a marked cop car. We can't stay in this alley."

"Where are we supposed to go, you dressed like that? You couldn't have grabbed a change of clothes."

"No. Are you insane? I grabbed the money. I only thought about the money. And the kids, of course."

"You're going to prison because of the kids."

"The timing was bad. Those kids were in wheelchairs."

"And we're going to be in prison."

Sirens shocked the day. We huddled together in the wet, dark alley. Lindsey held onto me, making me sick to my stomach.

"There are always sirens," I whispered stupidly to her.

"My God . . . prison!" Lindsey gasped.

"Don't say that word. Stay calm! I'm sorry, but it was a once in a lifetime grab at the dough; nobody saw me do it."

"Oh, come on; how could they not?"

We crouched in the greasy alley until an ambulance passed, its awful cry dying in the soft roar of the city. We both breathed again.

"We have to get out of here," I said. "We have a lot of cash, we can find a place to hold up—some place that doesn't ask questions."

"When they see you, they're going to ask questions."

"What can I say? I had no time. I probably scared those kids to death running away like that."

"You panicked."

"You're damned right I did! And so did you. Now we'll have to go out there and find a place. There should be a lot of cheap hotels around here."

"Oh, God . . ."

"We can't sit here in this filthy alley. We have to go out there."

I took her hand and we pushed out of the shadows into the hot sunlight. The masses of people stared at me as we rushed past them. They stared at me, they laughed at me.

A well-dressed Wall Street fellow was choking he was laughing so hard at me.

"Think of the children in wheelchairs, you prick!" I yelled at him. I gripped the bag full of money at my side. I thought of the children, the momentary joy on their faces. I thought that this was a bad day to wear my clown suit and makeup. It was not wise to carry this much cash in the bad side of New York, with the authorities looking everywhere for you, dressed as a full clown—let the reader be advised.

"Be quiet!" Lindsey trotted me forward, her face terrified and humiliated at the same time. Her eyes blinked like hummingbirds. "We have to get off this street. Look for a boarding house or something. We have to get off the streets."

"We have money. We're still in America."

"Oh, God, your makeup is running."

"Okay, don't panic."

"No!" Her voice went off like a bomb. I cried in my heart. Lindsey looked behind her at the police car that was crawling behind us. "We're dead. We're going to prison."

I pushed her along the hot sidewalk, my eyes glancing at the police car that was following close behind us. I knew that I was the most conspicuous figure on this sidewalk, a pure clown in suit and make-up who only wanted to see the kids laugh, and then get off with enough stolen dough to give us an early retirement. I asked God to forget the stolen money and think about the kids in the wheelchairs, how they laughed.

"You had to be a clown. Now we're going to prison and we'll never have anything," Lindsey said.

I glanced over at the police car, the officer leaning out his window, studying me.

"There's a place right up there, see? The Pink Hotel."

"They're slowing down. This is the end."

It was true. I wiped the paste off my face, my hands white, shaky.

I'm a crook. I stole money and tried to get away with it. Beyond all that, the kids laughed.

"Well, it's over." I looked at the neon sign of the hotel; Its sign dead and unblinking, sad like the kids who laughed. I looked at the police car; the officers studied me. Prison. Humiliation, shame. Losing all the money.

"I'm sorry, Lindsey."

"You had to be a clown."

"The kids laughed."

The two policemen stared at the sidewalk.

"Look at the guy in the clown suit."

"He's the right size. He's with a young woman with brown hair."

"A guy in a clown suit? He'd run with the money wearing a clown suit. No, this definitely ain't the guy."

A Day In The Madhouse . . .

"SPE on S-5!" the loudspeaker blared out, startling the calm of our downstairs ward, S-2.

"SPE on S-5!" Me and Greg ran out of S-2 into the green concrete hall, Greg's eyes fierce at the prospect of a safe fight with plenty of back-up.

"SPE on S-5!"

That meant Special Psychiatric Emergency on the ward Security #5, the worst ward in the Security Building. Our feet pounded down the hall, psychologists and social workers getting out of the way. Our feet pounded up the concrete stairs—toward what?

Greg (an asshole), was the faster runner and wanted to show off in a fight in which he couldn't be badly hurt. He got to the steel door first, swiped his badge down the electric lock and we barreled into a ball of confusion that rolled on the green carpet: S-5 technicians were already wrestling with the two patients trying to kill one another, Glen Hedgecock and Clarence Maze. I knew them both. Clarence was a huge muscled brute the color of strong coffee; he had beaten his girlfriend to death.

Glen was a skinny schizophrenic the color of milk, who had stabbed his college professor to death. Clarence was a giant with arms like railroad ties; but I knew that it was skinny Glen who'd started the fight, and that there was no reason behind the fight.

I saw a 100 pound young student nurse dive into the fight, and it gave me the courage to dive into it. I've worked in the mental hospital for 30 years, with big fat macho technicians and hard little nurses. It's the hard little nurses who have the true courage. I instinctively grabbed for Glen's legs, wrapping them as hard into my arms as I could.

Glen would attack anyone his voice-ears told him to. No matter that it was a murderous god of muscle built in a penitentiary.

I knew that what truly scared the big guys from the pen was not the squawky well-built cons trying to get courage with their mouths, their jive. What scared them was the skeleton madman who knew nothing of bigness or mean-ness or toughness.

What scared everybody (me too), about Glen Hedgecock, was unpredictability. If you know that a mental patient has been building up to violence, you expect it. There was no expecting anything with Glen. He had been playing cards with Clarence only minutes before he attacked him, swinging and kicking. He had flown into me like that before. All I remember is a crazy skeleton slamming my face while I was looking at the butt of a student nurse. He broke my cheekbone and dislocated my shoulder—and he Liked me.

He liked Clarence too. Clarence could never get over the mad things that Glen would say. That's probably why Clarence didn't crush his skull in the fight.

I saw a little 98 pound student nurse fly right into the fight, and so of course I followed her. In a situation like this I always go for the legs, trying to wrap them into me and hold on like a bronco rider. There were finally enough of us to get them apart and into restraints. I've worked for years with Social Workers, Psychologists, Psychiatrists, Mental Health Technicians and Nurses; I've found that it's the Nurses who dive into the violence first.

Clarence got calm fast, so we let his massive arms out of the restraints. Glenn Hedgecock, whose face was pretty much cracked open, was still so wild that he had to be wrestled into full-bed restraints and put on Homicide Watch. After his injuries were attended to by the nurse, he lay on the steel cot and sponge mattress in the Seclusion Room, his smashed mouth pouring out madness.

The Psychologist Dr. Woods showed up on S-5, a stern knight (after the violence was over), who would get to the bottom of this outburst of violence. He was a thirtyish gink who dressed in severe suits and ties and brought sweats to the hospital so that he could jog and lift weights down in the gym on his lunch break. He was very dedicated to the paperwork and documentation that was required in the field of mental health. He was probably writing a book.

After chatting with the cute young student nurse, Dr. Woods marched bravely down the hall to Seclusion, where Glen Hedgecock lay safely strapped down, like Da Vinci's perspective man sketch. S-5 calmed; the atmosphere settled back into its despair. I smiled at fate: before I could get to his legs, Glen had kicked Greg in the face, and now he was being treated by a nurse down whose blouse he stared.

I accompanied Dr. Woods back and unlocked Seclusion. The young student nurse was with us, and Dr. Woods assumed an air of importance, as if to say, Stand Back,

I'll handle this.

There wasn't anything to handle. Woods could ask Glen anything he wanted, and it would make no sense. Maybe he tried, I don't know. I know that I spent a hundred times longer with Glen than he had.

"They say you attacked Clarence . . . Maris?"

"Maze," I said.

"Thank you. Clarence Maze."

"I did," Glen said, staring at the psychologist.

"Why did you attack him?"

"I'm crazy." Glen stared at the psychologist.

"That's the only excuse you have, Glen?"

I was astounded by the question. Glen was too. He stared at the psychologist as if some horror was due him in the future. He wanted to destroy this psychologist who wanted to help him. Glen's utter madness did scare Dr. Woods; I could see his Adams apple bounce.

"I'm crazy," Glen said.

These things happen, and it's a damned shame. I worked with insane men for thirty years. I tried to feel some of their never-ending pain and hopelessness; I was the first to find some of them dead, with Walmart bags tied round their necks with belts. But I never ventured too far into the absolute pain and fear of that world. When madness exploded, I tried to end it and earn my paycheck.

In this place there is madness and violence, despair and rage. I know these guys, and their insanity. I'm not really afraid of any of them. In order to do my job well, I must explore their world; I have to taste madness in order to help them.

That's what scared me.

What Became Of Mary?

No one even knew the young man's name. The police had found him under a bridge in Lincoln, Nebraska. He was ranting, and it was plain that he had schizophrenia and was suffering a major spell of insanity.

In the security ward at the State Hospital, he astounded even the older nurses with his level of madness. Dr. Martin examined him as he lay in Seclusion, strapped up in full-beds to the metal cot.

"Can you tell us who you are?" he asked the wild-eyed young man.

"Albert Einstein proved that energy and matter are the same. Hispanic women pose naked. Asian girls just turned legal. Russian drillers have found what they say is hell. Stephen King is a novelist who specializes in horror. Gold reached a high of 1,560 dollars an ounce. I need to get to Mary."

"Can you say your name?" Dr. Martin asked.

"General George Custer was killed at the Little Big Horn. Threesomes and Swingers. Girls barely legal.

Over Forty. Diamonds are formed out of pressurized carbon. Osama Bin Laden is still alive. I need to get to Mary."

"Who is Mary?"

"Silver has reached 30 dollars an ounce. The British army burned the American White House in the War of 1812."

Dr. Martin turned away and rolled his eyes at the nurse. "Put him on one-to-one. Keep him in the full beds, but do one hour evaluations and call me if you think he's calm enough to come out of restraints."

The young man ranted until the drugs took over. He lay in seclusion mumbling disconnected trivia. Mental Health Technicians, who were to watch him, quickly made a game of asking him questions, all of which he could answer.

"He's like a human computer," one said.

The next day, three official men appeared, with legal papers giving them the right to take the man away to a private asylum. Dr. Martin read the judge's order. He looked at the men. This insane patient was obviously well-connected. His family—or guardians—wanted a private place, not the state mental institution. All right; be that as it may. Technicians escorted the young man to a black SUV in the parking lot.

Now he was the property of the three men in black suits. They drove off with the madman and no one ever found his body.

Mr. Sayne (that was funny), called the lab: "We found Joe," he said.

"Where?" the voice asked. No one knew his name or had ever laid eyes on him. They just called him the voice.

"Under a bridge in Lincoln, Nebraska—if you can believe that."

"End him."

"All right," Mr. Pell spoke up, "I'll handle it." He looked at the third man in the trio, Mr. Sloan. "It'll be putting him out of his misery." To the speakerphone voice, he said, "We'll get the body to you."

"We only want the head," the voice said.

"All right," Mr. Pell said. "The head it is."

"Get completely rid of everything else. What about Mary?"

"The control chip in her is stronger," Mr. Sloan said. "She hasn't shown any sign—"

"She escaped the Institution. She broke her contract. That indicates a problem; we want no problems."

Mr. Sayne spoke up: "We don't think Mary will present any threat—"

"Where is she?" the voice interrupted. "How did she escape?"

"We're not sure," Pell said. "She has an ex-husband living here in Nebraska; some kind of Uni-bomber weirdo; that's where we're going. It ain't no coincidence that we got Joe here. He was triangulating her."

"Why can't we?"

"We can, but it's intermittent," Sloan said. "The signal keeps cutting out."

"Is that a sign that her control chip is going to blaze out, like Joes?"

"Not sure," Sayne spoke up. "What should we do when we get her?"

"We can't take any chances," the voice said.
"Understood," said Pell.

Sebastian Powell watched the helicopter. He was in the woods on his 50 acre farm near Dexter, Nebraska, where 500 pot plants grew in strategic islands of sunlight.

He was a paranoid by nature (and occupation), and any sound of aircraft squirmed his stomach. This helicopter really worried him, and he power-walked up toward his farmhouse, rolling up water hose as he went. The damn thing wasn't moving on, it was hovering. Not good, not good. He saw that it wasn't a police copter, or DEA. He had beaten a marijuana rap years ago by proving that hemp grew everywhere in Nebraska, even on land owned by the judge in the case. But that had not, of course, eased his paranoia, nor made him popular with the sheriff's department.

He squatted down on the pasture and pulled up his binoculars. It didn't seem to be any official helicopter. Anyway, they wouldn't spend the money to send one after a nobody like him. Why the hell was it just hovering up there?

Sebastian Powell was truly a nobody; by choice a man almost totally off the grid. No cell phone, no computer, no bank account. Everything untraceable cash. He had been married to a woman who was the opposite, a techno addict, and she had made him realize that he was not equipped to live in this new world of Facebook, Internet and "Connectedness".

Mary was a brilliant computer scientist, and he was a scrubby pot grower. One day they got into a mega argument and Sebastian was stupid enough to remind her that his "plant business" brought them ten times the money (cash!) than her job at Futurecom. She walked out of his life, and the Odd Couple thing was over.

But it wasn't.

Sebastian crouched down in the prairie grass and watched the copter hovering over his farm. Then suddenly a far-off scream startled him. He dropped the field glasses and looked over at a figure running toward him. What the—?

"My God," he said.

The woman wore blue jeans and a red Nebraska tee shirt. The one he had bought for her on the day the Cornhuskers beat the hated Penn State. Her hair was brown, and tied back in a ponytail. She ran desperately up from the gravel county road, where he saw she had abandoned a car. He stared at her, not believing. She was terrified.

"Mary?"

She ran up to him and she looked up at the helicopter. "Seb! I'm sorry! I'm sorry!"

"What?"

"They're after me, Seb! I think they want to kill me!"

"Who's after you?"

"Futurecom! I have to get out of here!"

"Futurecom?"

"I have to get out of here!" Mary stared at the hovering copter. "I'm sorry—I didn't have anywhere else to go. They want to kill me, and now they'll kill you! I'm sorry!"

Old military training took over when Sebastian spotted the black SUV spraying gravel into his drive.

He jumped up, grabbed Mary and dragged her to the farmhouse.

"We need to get out of here!" she screamed.

"Too late for that. We need to get to my rifle."

He took her hand and rushed her to the farmhouse, where a tiny Chihuahua began yapping in alarm.

"Malone!" Mary said. "You've still got Malone."

"Of course," Sebastian said. He got a semi-automatic rifle out of the closet, checked the clip, and stepped out on the porch. Mary collapsed in a trembling pile on the couch, Malone jumping onto her lap. She rubbed his bat-like face. "Oh Malone," she said. "You're still here; and you still think you're a pit bull." She flinched at the sound of gunfire from the porch. "Seb! What are you doing?"

He came into the house. "No law against shooting a gun into the air."

"You were shooting at that helicopter."

"Be quiet, Malone. You've heard gunfire before."

"He's shooting at the copter," Mr. Sayne said, his voice jittery.

"No, he's shooting towards the copter," Pell said.

"Back off," said the voice on the speaker phone. "We've got her; now just wait."

"This won't be a problem," Mr. Pell said. "He gets scared enough, he'll give her up. He's a paranoid pot head. And she's just an ex-wife."

"The pothead is an ex-Navy Seal. They don't get scared."

"Ex means ex."

"No, it doesn't. Back the chopper off and wait. Neither one of them has a cell phone or land line. We've got her in the air and on the ground."

"We should at least send them a message," Pell said.

A pause. "All right," the voice said. "Make it a brief one."

"Looks like they're backing off," Seb said. "Malone, be quiet." He looked at Mary. "What the hell is this?"

"I'll have to explain later. Now we have to try and get out of here."

"Futurecom. The company you work for is trying to kill you."

"And now they want to kill you. Is there some way we can get out of here?"

"Mary—"

Machine gun bullets spattered the house. Sebastian dove onto Mary and rolled under the couch. Bullets splintered the house, riddled drywall, splashed glass pictures and shot cotton out of the couch.

"Jesus Christ!" Sebastian pushed Mary down and grabbed the rifle. He crawled over to one exploded window. The black SUV roared away down the gravel road. He aimed to shoot at it, but thought better. Let them wonder if they'd got the job done.

"Tell me what the hell this is about." He turned to Mary, who lay on the floor holding Malone.

"It has nothing to do with your—growing operation. It's a lot worse. We have to get out of here or we'll both die. I'll explain later."

Sebastian was never one to procrastinate—not when automatic weapon fire had riddled his house. "Come on." He jerked Mary off the floor and, shouldering the rifle, pulled her out the door. "Come on, Malone; you have to go too."

"Where?" Mary asked.

"We have to make it to the woods. I have an exit strategy. For the cops, not your computer company."

"Not computer company, Advanced Research Facility. And more." Mary blinked her eyes. "They're coming back."

Sebastian stared down the gravel road. "How do you know?"

"I'm reading their GPS."

"What?"

"Trust me—we have to get out of here!"

"Okay."

He rushed them toward the woods across about a thousand yards of pasture. Malone skittered with them, barking at the noise from over the hill. The black SUV reappeared.

"It won't do any good hiding in the woods," Mary said.

"We're not going to. Trust me," Sebastian said as they plunged into the trees.

He led her into a mass of plum bushes, and Mary was astounded when Sebastian found a trap door hidden under mulch and leaves. A ladder leaned down into darkness. Seb crawled down into the earth and suddenly a battery-powered lantern beamed on, revealing a giant Hum Vee. "Climb down," he ordered. "Bring Malone with you."

Cradling the Chihuahua, Mary climbed down into a concrete bunker. She marveled at the big red Hummer. "My god!"

"Paid cash for it," he said. "My exit strategy against the DEA or worse. I never thought I'd be on the run from a computer company."

Mary frowned. "I'm afraid they're more than a computer company."

"Well, get in, and fasten your seatbelt."

Mary climbed into the Hummer, strapped herself down and clutched Malone, who was grinning excited at this unexpected adventure. Sebastian jumped into the driver's seat and fired the monster truck up. Mary closed her eyes and hugged the Chihuahua. She had instinctively escaped to Sebastian because she knew him; she knew he could be a very loose cannon; he was her only hope, because he was the most unpredictable man she had ever known. She had fallen in love with him because, with Sebastian, there was rarely a dull moment. He hated televisions and computers, he hated cell phones, he hated satellites—he even hated radios. And he was the most exciting man she had ever known.

"Hold on tight to Malone," he said. "And you might want to close your eyes."

She didn't close her eyes, but she wished she had. Sebastian gunned the Hummer and it roared up a ramp, burst out of the prairie and bounded into the woods. He steered it around the trees, and gunned it, and suddenly they were in prairie sunlight, racing across the grass toward the road. He looked into the rearview mirror.

"They're at the house—whoever they are."

They barreled down to a dirt trail and Sebastian gunned the Hummer onto the gravel road. They roared east as Mary, shaking with fear, hugged Malone.

"How'd you get to me?" he asked.

"I—I rented a car. It's on the road west of your house."

"Yeah, I saw it."

When they were on the highway going toward Lincoln, Sebastian said, "I guess you should give me some information now. Who are those people?"

"They belong to Futurecom."

"And why are they trying to kill us?"

"To protect a very secret project from being discovered."

"What project?"

"Me."

She studied the supplies in the SUV; an impressive hoard of survival gear filled every inch. Malone lay in her lap like a big mouse. She let out an exhausted moan. "I guess falling in love with a paranoid drug dealer finally paid off."

"I'm not a dealer, I'm a supplier. Mary, who are these people?"

"They're following us." Mary blinked her eyes and seemed to go into a quick trance. "I'm reading their GPS."

Sebastian glanced behind him. "I don't see them back there. How do you know they're following us?"

"I told you: I can read their GPS."

"And they can read your brain. I get it."

He turned abruptly onto a gravel road and gunned the Hummer over a hill. At Connestoga Lake he turned in and found a hidden parking spot screened from the road by a dense stand of cedar trees. They were almost on the lake, where slushing shallows lapped at patterns of moss. Big bass lurked there, under the moss. You got them with poppers, and they gave a very good fight. At night, the catfish rolled in, big ones. He drew a pistol out of the glove box. He looked at Mary.

"What did they do to you?"

"It was my fault," she said. "I volunteered."

"For what?"

"To be the most knowlegeable person on earth. I would say the smartest, but it turns out that wasn't true." She stared away at the lake. "I volunteered to be implanted with a special chip we were researching. It's in my brain."

He gave her his squinched-eyes look that had always infuriated her: "They put a computer chip in your brain. Jesus, Mary—am I dreaming this?"

"No; and you didn't smoke too much weed. Well, maybe you did, but you're not dreaming. Ask me any question."

"What?"

"Ask me a question that I can't possibly know the answer to."

Sebastian stared away, clearly upset. "Ask you a question . . ."

"Not a personal one; a trivia one."

"Okay . . . you always hated history: who commanded the union forces at the Battle of Gettysburg?"

Mary blinked her eyes twice: General George Meade."

"What Nebraska governor and senator received the Medal of Honor when half his leg was blown up in Viet Nam?"

Two eye-blinks: "Bob Kerry. These are stupidly easy, Seb. It doesn't matter. The trick is, I can access the Internet with my mind. And that's a lot of knowledge."

He looked at her. "Where is the world's largest corn maze?"

"About two miles west of here."

Sebastian shuddered. He shook his head, as if to wake up. "What's with the eye blinks?"

"It's like tapping a mouse, or a keyboard. Only a lot quicker. This is the quantum leap I've worked all my life for; this will change humans and human society forever."

"It doesn't sound so great to me at the moment," he said. "So, you can go onto the Internet—real fast. Just by using your brain."

"The speed of light." Mary rubbed at Malone, who wriggled in her lap. "I can access all information on the Internet at the speed of light!"

"Mare—why would you let them stick some computer chip in your brain?"

She stared away. "I can't make you understand—I never could. It's all about human evolution, and taking it to the next level."

"The next level seems to be trying to kill us."

"I'm sorry. It was a monumental project I got caught up in. I thought I would be a pioneer, an explorer—the first to make the leap. There were two of us; Joe was actually the first."

"Joe."

"A computer scientist at Futuretech. He volunteered and went first, before they had perfected the control chip."

"So what happened to him?"

"The control chip failed. He went insane, and they killed him."

There were the squinch-eyes again. "Mare—what kind of crazy shit is this?"

"There has to be a control chip," she said. "A way to control access to the Internet with your mind; otherwise the Internet will pour uncontrolled into your brain, like a dam burst or something. That happened to Joe."

"Is it going to happen to you?"

"I don't know." She hugged Malone and began sobbing. The dog whined and glanced fearfully at Sebastian.

"Okay," he said. "Well, I guess the only thing that matters right now is staying alive." He looked at Mary hugging the Chihuahua. "Right?"

"Right," she said. "I'm sorry."

"You should be. But no matter. I have to figure out how to kill the guy with the rifle."

"What?"

"And hope he's the only one out there. He is the only one out there—right?"

"Yes. He's the killer; the other two are the finders. Believe me, Seb, they'll run from you."

"I don't believe anything. But that guy took a shot at me, and I'm going to take a shot at him." He handed her the pistol. "You know how to use this."

"You made sure of that."

"Remember I once told you—"

"Some day it might save your life. I remember. But they're here, Seb."

The black SUV halted at the entry to Connestoga Lake. Sebastian slipped out of the Hummer and into the woods. The SUV crept cautiously into the recreation area. Mary saw the large man jump out and sprint, rifle in hand, into a mess of willow trees along the lake. That would be Pell.

The SUV spun round and roared back out onto the gravel road, out of danger. Mary grabbed Malone in one hand and the pistol in the other, and lay down in the Hummer. It would only take Pell a second to spot this monster truck. She ventured up just to glance round the willow and cedar woods. She couldn't spot Sebastian. She looked at the SUV standing on the road. Bobby had said they were Sayne and Sloan. Mary didn't know them, but she had heard of them: they were the team to find her, no matter where she ran, and leave the dirty work to Pell. She dropped back down with Malone.

"You hear a sound, Buddy, you start barking."

There was very little sound. The wind blowing in the trees, bringing the muddy smell of the lake. Malone's ears were stabbed up.

What the hell is this? His eyes asked her. She closed her own eyes and tried to get over the horror that had tormented her body and mind for many days. A bullet in the heart; but that might be the easiest way out of this. What happened to Joe was worse.

Malone growled; his mouse-face danced at the open window of the Hummer. Seb was a pit bull guy; but when they went to the Humane Society five years ago this one dinky Chihuahua growled and snapped at him, making both of them laugh. A puppy that could sleep in a tea cup. She never thought that she would ever see Malone again. Or Sebastian.

"What is it, Baby?" she whispered.

Malone growled and put on his mean face. Mary gripped the pistol, made sure the safety was off. She had shot this particular pistol many times, wanting to please her husband. Now, these impossible years later, to be here in Nebraska with a miracle in her brain, holding this almost-forgotten pistol. "I know everything," she whispered to Malone. "I can get any kind of information just by thinking it. How can that help us now?"

A soft "PAT!" near the Hummer made her jump. Another "PAT!"

She had seen the silencer on Seb's rifle. She snuck her head up. Sebastian was slipping through the trees. He got into the driver seat and saw in the rearview mirror the SUV on Connestoga Road.

"What happened?" Mary crept up from the floorboard.

"I popped the guy."

"You—"

"He was trying to kill us."

"But—"

"Mary, he was trying to kill us. Now we have to deal with those guys." He started up the Hummer and gunned the engine. The SUV roared away toward the highway. "The guy was good; he found a big log to lie behind. But he shifted and I saw the rifle. Then he stuck his head up—"

"I don't want to know!"

"All right. Oh, shit. There's our whirly bird."

The helicopter hovered out of range. Sebastian roared the Hummer out onto the gravel road and took the opposite way the SUV had. The road, Mary remembered, snaked west toward Milford, about twelve miles away. The helicopter followed them.

"They're spending a lot of money trying to get you," he said.

"Trying to keep a secret," she said. "You know the secret; they probably know that."

"So I have to die too."

"I'm sorry, Seb. You were the only one who . . ."

"Who's stupid enough to help you."

Mary blinked her eyes. "Bobby's calling me." She went into a trance, then came out.

"They drove back into the lake," she said. "The two other guys, Sayne and Sloan. They drove back into the lake."

"Who the hell is Bobby?"

"He's my friend on the inside; he interfered with the tracking signals. He's risking his life every time he contacts me."

"They're going back for their pal. Sorry, but I know I popped him dead. He's the one who shot up my house. Mary, we have to go to the cops with this. We need to contact the police as soon as we can."

"Let's wait," Mary said.

"Wait . . . for what?"

She blinked her eyes and went back into the trance.

"Mare, we need to call the police—"

"No. Bobby says to wait."

"Bobby says—where is this Bobby?"

"He's at Futuretech, in Cleveland."

"In Cleveland. And he says to wait."

"He's risking his life, like we are. Without him I would have died over a week ago. He helped me escape."

"Escape from Futuretech."

"Bobby told me to wait."

"Bobby says to wait."

They drove in silence for many minutes, down the familiar gravel road. Mary stared at the green prairies and creeks passing in old memories. The soft and simple hills of Nebraska. Sebastian skirted Milford and found a very primitive dirt road that fell into a witchlike hollow of oak and ash trees. He put on the brakes suddenly and shut off the Hummer. They could hear the helicopter chopping the air, but they couldn't see it.

"I don't think they're going to drop anybody out of that yet. They're just keeping an eye on us."

"God . . . what have I done?"

"I don't know," he said. "Right now I don't care. You have this great chip in your brain. How is that going to help us?"

"I'm not sure. It may."

"It may. Why is this Bobby trying to keep us from contacting the police?"

"I'm not sure. But I think we should wait; give it fifteen minutes."

Mary went into her short trance. "Oh, Jesus. They left the body behind. They left Pell."

"Why would they leave him? They want to keep this quiet."

"Bobby says they took his rifle."

"I don't get this. This is crazy, Mare. We need to go to the cops and tell them everything—except about my farming operation. Okay?"

Mary held onto an excited Malone. He was a Chihuahua who always thought he was a Doberman. She stared out at the trees, the creek hollow, the elfin shadows. "Why are we parked here?"

"They can't see us. We're sitting here enjoying the scenery, and that chopper is going to run low on fuel pretty soon, and they'll have to go somewhere to refuel. Where did the SUV go?"

"Away from us, toward the highway."

"I thought so." Sebastian stared up at the canopy of trees. "They didn't take his body, but they took his rifle. We need to get to the police, Mare. If they bust me, well it's better than—"

"No wait. Please wait. Oh God, you killed a man! Are you all right?"

"Don't worry about me, I'm having the time of my life," Sebastian said grimly. "I suppose I could have let him kill us, but that didn't seem prudent. Now, I'll wait about ten more damn minutes; then your boyfriend better tell me why I don't call the police."

"He's not my boyfriend. Bobby isn't into girls." Her eyes blinked furiously: "They're moving fast. I found out the second I got out of there that they move fast. I signed papers and took vows—and I violated them."

"Why do they want to keep this so secret?"

"I don't know. We were never told that."

"Well, there they go. Bye bye, pricks."

Mary heard the helicopter chatter away. Silence spooked in, making the forest around them that much more sinister. She stared away at the windblown trees. "We can't stay here, Sebastian. I'm so sorry!"

"It's pretty obvious that we can't stay here. It'll take them about an hour to fuel up that bird and get back on us. This time they might drop a sniper. So where do we go?"

She gave him a frightened stare. "I don't know."

"You're the smartest person on the planet, and you don't know."

"Off the grid." She looked back at the camping gear Sebastian had stored in the Hummer. He of all people would sneer at Armageddon. "I'm sorry. They can't track us if we go where there are no satellite signals."

"Where the hell is that?"

"I'm trying to find out." She blinked her eyes. "We have to keep going west. I'm sorry for all of this." She petted the Chihuahua she used to play with, Malone attacking her hand clothed in a thick wool sock, and how his needle teeth ripped into the sock, and how tiny he was, and how ferocious. That safe, good feeling of the farm came back to her. "I'm sorry, Malone," she said.

"Okay, west it is. But now it's nine minutes before I call the police."

They drove the winding road west. Mary rubbed at Malone and stared at the cornfields and hills of alfalfa that passed by. Bobby told her that they had cut off Joe's head and got rid of the body. Bobby said he thought they were going to do that to her. Bobby, the one she could always trust.

I volunteered. I vowed that I would never leave Futurecom without written permission. I signed my name to every paper, wanting desperately to get into the center of the web, where the miracles were happening. Then Joe's control chip failed, and Bobby came into my room and said you have to get out now.

"I don't know that much about Futurecom. They didn't want me to know, and that was okay with me," Mary said. "I knew they were doing what I'd always dreamed of doing; putting the knowledge of all mankind into a single brain."

"Yours."

"You don't like the future, Seb. You never liked reality."

He gave her one of his looks. "I think I'm handling reality pretty well so far. You're down to seven minutes, Mary."

She blinked her eyes. "They moved faster than us. God, I'm sorry!"

"Sorry—what?"

She blinked her eyes. Sebastian wondered if it was Morse Code, which he knew. But if it was, it was too fast for him to read. "They've already contacted the Lincoln police," she said. "They reported witnessing the murder of Andrew Pell, at Connestoga Lake."

"What?"

"They gave the police our description and license number."

"Jesus—what!"

"The Lincoln police, the Nebraska State Patrol, they're all looking for you—a suspected marijuana grower. Bobby says they're going to find Pell's body and blame it on you."

"No—no! We're going to the cops right now and we're going to clear this up."

"Clear what up, Seb? You killed him."

"I shot a sniper who was about to kill us—to kill you. I'm not going to take some murder rap."

Mary blinked her eyes. "Bobby's following them. They're headed into Lincoln, probably to talk to the police. They're setting you up, Sebastian. I had no idea they were so fast and ruthless. I should have." She blinked her eyes and said, "I'm reading the e-mails, Seb; they're setting you up. I'm sorry! This can all happen so fast!"

"That's it; I'm calling the cops. The first pay phone we come to, I'm calling the cops."

"There are no pay phones anymore."

"Beaver Crossing's just up the road. I'll call the cops from the café."

"God, Seb; how can this be happening?"

He looked over at her. Life seems to die easy. Love dies hard. Or maybe the songs are true: it never dies. He was worried about her, she was cracking. He had learned long ago not to go into the brain-shock that kept telling you a situation couldn't be happening—that somehow you'd wake up. He sighed.

"I know a place. Lucky for us it's west, about 600 miles."

"Where?"

"Google this, chip-girl: Iron Lake, Utah."

She blinked her eyes. Sebastian watched her go into what seemed to be, from her blissful eyes, a beautiful world, as she held a worried Malone. He needed to keep her busy, her mind occupied.

"Intermittent cell phone service," she said. "A lot of iron, and it's an isolated place."

"I know. But first, I call the cops."

"And they'll arrest you for murder. And Futurecom will find a way to kill you. And then they'll kill me, and then they'll kill Malone, and then—"

"Mary, calm down. You can't be a spazoid on me now. I have to call the cops."

"And give yourself up?"

"No, not even close."

Sebastian pulled into the Beaver Crossing Café and made his call. Then he sprinted into the Hummer and they roared off.

"What did they say?"

He looked at her. "Not much. But I made sure they recorded the call."

"Now they know where we are—where the call came from."

"I know. And all the folks here in Beaver Crossing are going to remember my Hummer."

"That means we're going to get arrested."

"These dicks from Futurecom; they're good. Get the local authorities to nail us. But when that happens, they can't let you live long. What they're doing is to try and get me out of the picture. I'm a drug dealer murderer, I kidnapped you. You go free and I'm in a cell. They'll have you alone. They don't care if I rot in prison or die. It's you they need. I tell them what I know and they're going to think I'm copping an insanity plea."

"So you're going to turn yourself in?"

"Hell no. You Questmap the dirt roads going west. We don't want to go straight west, we want to meander. Next we have to block your GPS signal."

She stared at him. "How do you know about Questmap? You're not even on the net."

"I read books. How do you block their signals? If they've got your brain tracked, it won't matter where we go."

"Bobby." She blinked her eyes.

Sebastian followed the dirt road that twisted down out of Beaver Crossing. He had hunted pheasants on this road. Nobody lived down here, and if it rained this road would stick a tank in its mud. It was dry now, and the Hummer rolled over the bumps and grooves as if they weren't there. He looked at the sky for signs of the helicopter.

"We have to keep them from tracking you."

"I know, I know." Mary's eyes tranced. "Okay. Bobby can block the GPS signal."

"That's good."

"But only for a while."

"What?"

"He's risking his life doing this."

Sebastian stared out at the grey dirt road. It was only to get near Iron Lake, ditch the Hummer so it couldn't be found, then go on from there. It didn't feel like a great plan.

"At some point, Mary, we're going to have to go feral."

She stared at him. She rubbed Malone. "Somehow I think you're good at that."

He smiled. "Remember when we went camping? How much fun you had? How you enjoyed it?"

"No, I didn't enjoy it. I didn't have fun. There were bugs and creatures and I had to take a crap around bushes."

He grinned at her. "You had fun. But now we're going to have to do it for real. And we'll need to go on offense."

"What are you talking about?"

"Number one, you have to use your power to go viral. You need to tell the world what's in your brain, who put it there, and what they're trying to do about it. Get this thing out there, that's what they're afraid of. Use whatever power you have to get this story out, onto the—hyper space, whatever. Believe it or not, even I knew this thing was coming. I never imagined that it would be with you."

"I made promises to them. The world isn't ready—"

"Screw your promises. These people—from what I gather—want to kill us and cut off our heads to keep you secret. Our best weapon is to Not keep you secret. Can you do that?"

"Yes," she said. "What's Number Two?"

"Number Two, we disappear for as long as we have to, we go feral. We attack them, but we can't stay in one place to do it."

"That's right. Viral, then feral." She looked at him, scared. "What if the control chip fails, like it did with Joe?"

"I don't know," he said. "But it's not going to help us thinking about what can go wrong. How long can this pal Bobby keep us off the grid?"

Mary blinked her eyes. She turned pale. "He's not answering! That might mean they caught him. Oh, Bobby!"

"Calm down. That phone call I made to the Lincoln police might get them wondering."

Scanning the sky, Sebastian drove the big Hummer as far as the dirt road went; then he turned onto the nearest gravel road west. His ears were alert to the sounds of sirens or helicopters. He didn't know how this all came about, Mary coming back into his life like a strange scared robot. This explosion of danger. Professionals who wanted to kill him for no reason. He only knew that he was in his element.

"Are they still tracking us?"

"No. I think Bobby scrambled the signals."

"You think?"

"Sebastian, I don't know. Hold on, I'll try to find their signals."

Mary blinked her eyes, went into her trance. "No, they're cold. They're cold, Sebastian."

"Okay, good. For now. Mary, you have to concentrate on getting all this out to the Internet, and especially to the authorities in Nebraska. You have to spill your guts about this. That's what they're terrified of, that you'll spill your guts. That's why they want to kill you. You Do know why, so tell me the truth."

"Other corporations are doing this, experimenting with computer-brain symbiosis. We were only the first and the best."

"Well, there's a reason they want to make you disappear. There's a reason you needed to escape—wasn't there?"

"Yes. I'm an experiment that is illegal. I'm an experiment that's a felony. I knew that all along; I knew that from the beginning. But Seb; I needed to be a pioneer. To have the knowledge of mankind in my mind."

"That might help us out. I'll get us as close to Iron Lake as I can. But there's going to be a time when we have to go camping, like it or not."

"Oh, Malone." Mary hugged the little mouse-dog, who stuck his ears up and growled. "You don't know what's in my mind. I don't really know."

"Whatever it is, they want to stop it. That means they're afraid of it. They want to kill you, Mary, because they're afraid of what you can do. So start thinking of what you Can do. We need to get off defense and go to offense."

"Okay; this is a football game. My God, Sebastian, you killed a man."

"Forget that. Now you use your brain chip to give us an edge."

Mary tried to recover her nerves. She knew that her ex-husband had killed men before, long ago in the navy. He wasn't proud of it, but he wasn't ashamed.

"The Hummer will take us as far west as we can get. But at some point we're going to have to go feral."

That happened three days later. They were 50 miles east of Iron Lake when the copter appeared overhead. Sebastian veered onto a side road and parked in a deep canyon. Mary was exhausted. They hadn't showered for three days and she felt skanky and dead, like a used washrag.

"Oh God," she said. "I'm ready to die."

"No, you're not. Grab Malone. We're going camping."

Sebastian scooped up his rifle and shot at the helicopter until it sped away into the blue Utah sky. He piled the camping equipment onto the ground, then put the Hummer into neutral and pushed it over the edge of the canyon. Mary stared in awe as the big vehicle rolled down, bouncing crazy over rocks and boulders, and crashed into the boulders below. She couldn't believe this was happening.

"Oh God Oh God Oh God!"

Sebastian touched her on the shoulder. "Iron Lake is that way." He pointed west. "Now we go feral. Have you got your boyfriend yet?"

"He's not my boyfriend. Yes, I've got him back." Mary blinked her eyes, went into her trance. "Bobby thinks they're scared."

"Good." Sebastian shouldered some of their equipment. "You get the rest. It's going to be rough, Mare. That chopper's going to be coming back. We have to get down to those woods."

Mary looked down the grey slope at a mass of trees below. "Are you going to make it down there, Malone?"

"He will or he won't," Sebastian said. "Here, grab this stuff and follow me. We're going camping."

"Oh, God." Mary hefted the two bags and followed Sebastian down the rocky slope. She was in the true world again, and she hated it. Too many years had passed since Sebastian forced her into the wilderness where ticks and snakes and dirt and stink were. Staring at stones and a dust trail that led down into a forest. She wanted to go back to that world she ruled; Artemis galloping in the sparkling mazes and the clean electric air of hyperspace. A world clean of reality.

Being in the Internet was being in God. She blinked her eyes and contacted Bobby. They know where the Hummer is, she thought to him.

"I know," Bobby's voice said to her mind. "Sebastian's right; you need to get online and expose them. Tell everybody what's going on. You're queen of the Internet. You can attack them and expose them. That's your best weapon now; and that's what they're afraid of. I've got to leave."

A dead spot in her mind. Mary came out and looked at Sebastian.

"Good news?" He gave her his squinch-eye.

Mary was suddenly and strangely in love with him again, she didn't know why. It was some crazy, stinky thing from her past, before the implant. It was the familiar look he was giving her now. She gave him a love smile. "Come on, Malone, we're going camping again."

Sebastian smiled at her. His rifle lay across his big shoulders. He carried a tent and sleeping gear and all they would need. Mary carried the rest down the rocky slope. She smiled at Malone, who two-stepped down with them, his mouse-face stern and defiant against rocks and snakes twice his size.

They came to a forest at the bottom of the mountain. Malone skittered his way down around the rocks, Sebastian trudged next to her. She blinked her eyes and saw all the information about where they were. She didn't contact Bobby; she didn't want him to get into trouble, or worse. She smiled at the insanity that had brought her back to a sleeping bag in the wilderness. She smiled at her ex-husband, she smiled at Malone. "Feral," she said.

Sebastian grinned at her. "Those are good woods. We camp there; then we go west to Iron Lake."

"I'm sorry," she said.

"Good; keep saying that. Now we go camping. They know I'm going to shoot at their helicopter, and they know that we're not going to go down easy. I like it when you tell me you're sorry."

"Okay, I'll spill my guts to the Internet. I'll tell everybody what I am and what's going on. And nobody's going to believe it."

"You might be surprised. I'll bet it freaks out the helicopter people."

"But in order to that, we have to find a place where I can sit and be out of it for a while."

"Out of it."

"A place where you can stand guard. We can't get too close to Iron Lake before I attack, because I have to maintain satellite signal."

"Okay . . ." He stared around them. Just below was a hill of boulders high enough to scan the mountains, and indestructible from most angles. "Down there, in those boulders."

"Oh, God, Seb; what if there are rattlesnakes down there? Or scorpions?"

"Then our bad day will get worse. Just get ready to do your Internet thing."

They crawled down into the nest of boulders, and Mary immediately blinked her code and began sprinting through hyper-space. It was a glorious, drunken escape. She could die it was so beautiful and perfect. This was why she had done it, to see this unreal world not just on a screen, but in her mind. It was so wonderful scampering down the sparkling streets and alleys and roads and highways of pure silver electricity. A world that controlled so much and had so much power and—it didn't exist.

She was no longer feral; she was no longer of the painful physical world. That's why she loved this. She was Artemis sprinting through magic forests of infinite knowledge, where every turn revealed sparkling avenues into all of the knowledge of man. She dropped quick information into the most important web sites and chat rooms. Soon it was apparent that Futurecom had detected her, and would try to log onto her mind in order to circumvent their lost GPS signal. Never mind, she had planted a viral seed. She immediately blinked off.

Malone was lying protectively next to her. She had the weird thought that Chihuahuas are probably good snake killers. Sebastian was squatting up above, just behind a boulder, the rifle in his arms. Mary shuddered. She sighed at the true world she came back to.

Sebastian looked down, saw that she had returned. He came down to the nest of boulders and she hugged him.

"I'm scared," she whispered. "I'm scared that they'll do something to the control chip and send me down into insanity."

"Like Joe."

"Yes! And then I'll be some schizophrenic in some hospital, hopelessly insane, and you'll be a murderer serving life in the pen. That's their plan."

"I think their plan is to kill us both and cut your head off to send it back for evaluation," Sebastian said. "Your job is to keep sending everything out to the Internet. My job is to set up a camp site and get us to Iron Lake."

"I sent a lot out; but then they detected me."

"And when they detect you, they can find you."

"Yes."

"Well, they've already found us, so that's not a worry."

"I sent a lot out."

Sebastian prepared the campsite; then settled down in the woods. Mary blinked her eyes many times and sent their story to the Internet, even saying where she was. Only minutes later Bobby contacted her to let her know that Futurecom was going into a panic, that she'd better get off-line fast. She blinked off and watched

Sebastian settle back with his rifle, Malone rubbing against him.

"I never stopped loving you," she said.

He looked at her. "You left me. This was never good enough for you."

"I know. But I came back."

He smiled at her. "You did. You came back. But with some really serious baggage." Sebastian stared at the sky. "And our whirly-bird's back."

"Oh, God."

"It's keeping its distance." Sebastian took up his binoculars and studied the copter. "They might drop a sniper this time. I can't shoot the thing. I seem to be in enough trouble already." He looked at Mary. "I thought our pal Bobby had them blocked."

"It's intermittent. But I've got an idea. All the sudden I've got a great idea."

"What's that?"

"I plant a worm in their system. No, I plant a lot of worms."

"What the hell is a worm?"

"It's something that completely screws their system." Mary scratched Malone's back. Sebastian watched her; she was turning into a ninja before his eyes. "An incremental worm, that's what they're afraid I'm going to make, and unleash. And I can do it like pissing on bushes."

He grinned. "Pull the trigger then. That might be what gets us out of this."

"You're right. It's time we fought back. I attack them through the Internet, you try to keep us alive."

"Okay."

"From him." Mary pointed at the distant helicopter.

Sebastian took up his glasses and watched the helicopter. A cable dangled from its open bay, and a guy was lowered to the ground. He was in full gear, and carrying a high quality sniper's rifle. Sebastian marked the spot where the guy landed. He watched the bird to see if it would drop another one, but it sped away, its blades making "Chocka! Chocka!" echoes in the canyon. The sniper vanished into the far trees. It was getting dark, and Mary was exhausted. Sebastian fished a pair of night-vision goggles out of his pack and strapped them on.

"You get a little sleep," he said.

"I can't sleep. Are you crazy?"

"Well, curl up in a sleeping bag and just be quiet; and try to keep Malone quiet. Now we talk in whispers."

"That man out there—he's stalking us, isn't he?"

"Yes, he is. If you can't sleep, at least rest your eyes and your brain. If we make it through the night it's going to be a busy tomorrow."

Mary lay back in the gathering darkness. She couldn't resist blinking in and out of the Internet. "This place is Daniel Canyon. It was formed when a glacier went through."

"I wonder who Daniel was."

"I'm sorry, Seb." She sounded comatose.

"Try to get a little sleep."

Mary dove into the Internet, her safe place. Sebastian climbed away from the nest of boulders and found a good spot behind a fallen pine log. The guy they had dropped was not very good, or he didn't know Sebastian had night vision.

The guy made so much noise coming toward them that Sebastian wondered if he was a distraction, and they'd dropped another better killer behind him. Soon enough Malone's sharp ears heard the guy creeping out of the trees, and he startled the night with his gunshot barks.

Good. This is where we are, dead man. Keep coming.

He kept the scope of his rifle on the guy, who danced SWAT-like around the trees. Malone's loud bark was spooking him. He was cautious, but not very good. Probably ex army or mercenary who was being paid a lot of money by Futurecom.

Sebastian watched him creep closer, and when he stepped one fatal time out of the trees, Sebastian popped him twice in the neck. He couldn't hear past Malone's insufferable barking, and Mary trying to shut him up; but it was pretty sure the guy was gurgling to death down there. Best to make sure. Sebastian waited a few minutes until Malone went silent. He studied Daniel Valley. No sign that there was another.

My life's probably over anyway, he thought. Two men now dead, me on the run. Mary dead, Malone dead.

He lifted off the night goggles and breathed in the cool mountain air. So beautiful out here; not a bad place to die if you have to. It was so quiet that he could hear Mary whispering to the dog. It would have been nice bringing them here just to camp and enjoy the true world. In another time, of course. Now Mary had found the world she wanted. He had watched her face when she went into the cyber-world, how ecstatic it was. A world of magic. She never liked camping anyway.

Sebastian crept carefully down the slope to the guy in the trees. He was draped over a log. He's dead alright; and I killed him. Sebastian slipped on latex gloves and frisked the guy, but he knew he wouldn't find anything.

He crawled back up to the nest of boulders, Malone suddenly letting out explosive barks. Mary had the pistol on him as he came into the nest.

"I'm on your side, Mary. Remember?"

She seemed almost in a coma, her eyes wide, fixed in an exhausted horror.

"What happened?" she whispered.

"Mary, put the gun down. I popped him, that's what happened."

"Oh God!"

"Don't go spazoid!" he whispered savagely. "Malone, shut up!" He stared round the bouldered valley. The night was growing chilly, but he leaked sweat. He whispered mechanically to her: "I hope I scared them off for good this time. Now I'm a double killer, and as soon as you can do it, you need to get our story out. It might be the only way to save us. But now we both need to sleep."

"Is there another one out there?"

"I don't think so. Let's hope that if there is, Malone can give us a warning."

"I'm sorry—I'm so sorry!"

"You need to sleep, girl. Come here."

She lay shivering and moaning next to him and he covered her in the down sleeping bag. Finally she drifted into a troubled sleep. Malone settled down, and he could hear him snoring softly. Sebastian looked up at the glittering sky. He wondered how the world Mary went into could be more beautiful than this one. Maybe because that world was safe, and this one wasn't. He couldn't say he was afraid; fear had always come to him in hardness, like stale bread. His mind had always been able to put fear and uncertainty away and to just deal with what was. Like getting busted for growing. Well, this was turning out to be a quantum leap from that.

"What in God's name is going on?" the voice demanded.

"We lost Stephens," Mr. Sayne said. He traded looks with Mr. Sloan. They both knew their lives were on the line.

"She's starting to flit onto web sites. She's telling everything. And she wants to plant worms in the system. You know what that means."

"Yes, we know. But the Nebraska authorities are—"

"No. That was a mistake. You might have thought it a clever coup de grass; but it was a stupid mistake."

"We can get the Utah police—"

"No! We keep the authorities out of it for now."

"He's murdered two men."

"And the story must end there. I'm sorry you lost two of your men; I'm sorry we thought this would be easy, like with Joe. But what matters now is that we can Not let her go on and give out any more information and plant more worms. She's fast becoming a grave danger. What are they doing out there?"

"We're close to some mountains that might interfere with satellite signals."

"That means that she can't get online. But if she gets enough information out there and some of those geeks grab onto it, it might go viral."

"We're trying to prevent that, Sir."

"How!"

"We'll get them. But he's already killed two of our men. He's in his element, and most of the team is getting scared shitless of him. The pilot refuses to go anywhere near his rifle range."

"We're trying to calm everybody down," Mr. Sloan put in, because he felt he had to say something. He was head of security for Futurecom, the pay was great; but he had known that it was a dubious title at best. He had certainly not signed up for this. "We have a plan," he lied, looking over at Mr. Sayne.

"Shut down everything and wait for my orders," the voice said. "That's the plan for now. I think it's time that I meet with Mary and we end this thing."

"Meet with Mary?" Mr. Sayne didn't understand. "How—"

"Be quiet," said the voice. "Get our copter out of there, stand down and wait for future orders."

He didn't have to finish the sentence ("or else"). Sayne and Sloan traded worried looks. But they were relieved. Flying around this wilderness in the helicopter, each had wondered if the madman pot grower from Nebraska could shoot them out of the trees and rocks.

Sebastian was awake before sunrise, but he let Mary sleep. Malone woke up hungry, and Sebastian gave him some water and two beef jerkies; the second one the tiny dog only played with. Malone grinned at him like some little bat in a cartoon. The Chihuahua was feeling very much the tough guy on this adventure, and would probably try and fight one of the mountain coyotes who roamed in grey-and-white flickers along those slopes.

Malone would be a meager lunch. A tame mouse in the wilderness, but one with a Napoleon Complex.

Sebastian's plan had been to get right into the Iron Mountains, where Mary assured him they would not be able to track them with satellite signals. But after mulling it over, he thought it best that they stay here, in their boulder nest. Futurecom might be expecting them to go on the move. And while tracking signals might not work up there, they also would chop off the best weapon they had, Mary's Internet power. Signals were trying to kill them and signals were trying to save them. And Mary needed a day of rest.

The helicopter had disappeared, for the time being. Now there was only the soft morning breeze, still cold as it flowed down out of the mountains. The sun gradually crept up, a red god in the east.

Rest up here for a day and start traveling at night, he thought.

The Iron Mountains of Utah were even rockier than this place. He had been there many times, camping with rattlesnakes and cougars. A good place to hide. A good place to die, if it came to that. He wondered about this Bobby. Mary had indicated that he was her friend on the inside, and had hinted that he was gay. And he was risking his life.

Why?

Malone began grumbling, but it was only because Mary was talking in her sleep. She was a very restless pillow-mate, and sleeping with her had always been a semi-wrestling match. She was snoring loud now, but why care? They know where we are. They also know what we can do. Is that why they backed away? Did they back away?

He took up his field glasses and scanned this valley, as dawn unveiled light and shadows backed away. He was good with binoculars. Growing pot, they had always been his friend. He saw many coyotes trotting around the boulders and vanishing into trees. He saw a large deer nibbling on mountain leaves. He saw elk down in the valley below, where a wriggly stream ran. There was water for the trek that had to be done at night. Run from them in the night, then attack them in the day. Until you get to the Iron Mountains, then you find a place to wait them out.

He rubbed Malone's skintight hair. The little dog was skinny as a rat. They needed a valuable dog on this one, a black lab or better, a Doberman. Not a little rat who thought he was big, and could break your heart with his grin and his spunk.

"Bobby . . ." Mary said suddenly in her sleep. "Save me, Bobby."

Sebastian felt his stomach sink. He didn't know why. Her mind had the ability to go into hyper-space; did she do it in her sleep? She loved this Bobby, he thought he knew it.

But he only knew that after the nightmares she would settle into the most blissful sleep Sebastian had ever seen. Mary was drifting into hyperspace, even as she slept. She was doing it now, hugging a tired Malone as she went into that world.

He stared at the bright canyon, red and grey and tired green. He felt that he was finally at the end of his life. He had pulled the trigger on men, back in the day; it always seemed like a light going out. Was it? Is that how it'll be, just an instant blackness in these crazed mountains?

Mary finally woke up, sputtered and shook her head. She stared out of her messed-up hair. "What time is it?" she asked.

"Late morning."

She stared round at the mountain valley; she hugged the soft sleeping bag. "You said we had to leave at dawn."

"I changed my mind. Get some more sleep, Mary."

"Oh, you . . ." She lay back down in the sleeping bag, under the soft mountain grass. She was snoring before he knew it, and her eyes flickered under their lids. He watched her, hating himself for falling in love with her all over again. She was poison, she was a disaster. She was a curse that had shown up in his life when he didn't need a curse.

He loved her, god damn it. That was about it.

Mary slept as the sun grew hot and dry in the Utah sky. Malone finished off his second beef jerky and squiggled down to sleep. No sign of the helicopter, no sign of anything. Sebastian settled back and got some rest. He wondered if the Utah cops would climb down here and arrest him, but somehow he didn't think they would. He lay still for half an hour, then got up and put a solar marine meal out in the bright sun, scrambled eggs and bacon, hoping that would wake Mary up.

It worked. Soon her nose sniffed the bacon, and she jumped awake. "Seb! What time is it?"

"It doesn't matter," he said. "Good afternoon. I've decided we're staying here today. If we need to move, it should be at night. I'm not sure we have to move."

"They know where we are." She glanced around the mountain valley.

"They're going to know where we are no matter where we go. Now it's up to you to save us."

She crawled out of the sleeping bag, rubbed sleep from her eyes. She petted Malone, who was eyeing the bacon being cooked by the sun. "What's for breakfast, Mountain man?"

He smiled. "Scrambled eggs and bacon. If you have to pee, go down there in those bushes."

"How do you know that?"

"When we camp out you always need to pee when you wake up."

Mary needed to pee. She got the job done down in the fragrant bushes that grew everywhere on this slope, sharing terrain with the giant grey boulders and Utah dust. When she returned to their boulder nest Sebastian had a tin plate of scrambled eggs and bacon ready, and a canteen of water. Mary smiled at him; she was hungry.

"No buttered toast—sorry. Now eat." He went back to his study of the canyon, his field glasses sweeping the terrain. "Something is going on. They backed off."

She gobbled down the breakfast, and gave Malone her last bite of bacon. "This is like the old days," she said.

"Not exactly." He put down the field glasses and looked at her. "How do you feel when you go into that hyper world?"

"What?"

"I've seen your face when you go there. You want to be there and not here."

She looked down at the stubbly ground. "Yes. I want to be there."

"Why? Reality isn't good enough?"

"It's hard to explain. I guess I feel safe there, powerful. Here I feel helpless and weak."

"Well, when you feel up to it, you need to go back on the attack. Go in there and attack them with our story. That's our nuclear weapon."

She studied him. The sun was climbing hot in the sky, but Sebastian had set up a shade tent, and the breeze still blew cool from out of the far mountains. When she ran to him she was afraid of the future, and the past. Now there didn't seem to be any future or past. She petted Malone, who stood sniffing the air for danger, as if he was the grand protector.

"Just so you know: I made a mistake leaving you guys."

He smiled. "Good to hear. Now get in there and attack those bastards. I'll keep watch."

Mary blinked her eyes and dived into the Internet, into the sparkling world where she was a goddess. She spread the story of Futurecom; she planted worms in their system with a swirl of her wand—and then something strange happened. She was whisked into a blank website that had no name. Her cyber-self stood in blankness, and she felt terror.

Then the voice: "Hello, Mary. Finally we meet."

A figure appeared before her, a human form of sparkling electricity. She tried to get out, but some force prevented her. This is the end, she thought. They shut off the control chip and now I'm going to go helplessly insane.

"No, Mary," said the electric thing. "We're not going to make you insane. But we are going to shut off the control chip, and the main chip."

"The main chip." She looked at her hyper body. She was a form of spattering electricity. She was a goddess—yet somehow she couldn't control this, couldn't escape.

"You passed the test. Now you go back into reality. Now Sebastian must leave his rifle behind, free of fingerprints. That's the only thing that can save him."

"What?"

"I want to save you, Mary. And I want to save Sebastian. He must leave his rifle behind, free of fingerprints."

She stared at the voice; the voice of Futurecom. "I don't want to go back. Is it you Bobby?"

"We tried to kill you, to remove the head from your body. You found a way to prevent that, to attack us. Now there will be no more attacking. Don't plant worms, and you will live to see tomorrow. You got to explore this world, to be a goddess in this world; but now it's over."

"The main chip," her voice said.

"Say goodbye to it. Say goodbye to this world, Mary."

"No!" She felt herself swirling into a funnel of light and sparkles, falling not into but out of existence, away from this world she loved so much. She blinked her eyes furiously trying to get back in. She desperately clenched her eyes shut trying to go back in. But it faded, and when she opened her eyes Sebastian and Malone were there, watching her. Beyond were the real mountains of Utah.

"You okay?" Sebastian asked.

"I'm—I'm not sure." She felt the sudden deadness in her brain. She blinked her eyes, but they kept seeing the real world, the grey boulders, green witchgrass and the pine trees blowing softly in the wind. "I can't . . ." she said.

"Can't what?"

"I can't go there anymore. They shut off the chip. I didn't know he could do it. I should have known that he could do it."

"Who's he?"

"I don't know. The voice, that's what they called him."

"What does that mean?"

"I don't know. He came to me as a creature of electricity. I only know that my power is gone."

"You need to contact Bobby, find out what's going on."

"I can't, Seb. The chip is dead. And we don't have a computer. I put out what I could, I told our story. But now it's dead. I should have known they could do it."

Sebastian sat back and stared away. "They could have shut you off at any time," he said. "Why didn't they, before you could go in there and—"

"I don't know!" Mary rubbed her eyes as if she had an intense headache.

"It can only be because they wanted you to." Sebastian traded looks with the Chihuahua. Malone smiled at him, if a dog can smile.

"I think it's over," she said. "It's over."

"It's not over," Sebastian said. "They might not be after you, but they're after me."

"He said to leave your rifle behind, to wipe off all fingerprints."

"Leave my rifle behind. That's a good one."

"No. Leave it behind, and let's get out of here."

Sebastian sat and evaluated the situation. If they thought he was powerless without his rifle, they were wrong. Things were beginning to make sense, maybe. "Bobby says that?"

"I can't talk to Bobby anymore," Mary said. "They've shut me off completely."

"Okay, we'll play along." Sebastian wiped the rifle clean and lay it against a boulder. They relaxed in their boulder nest and waited. Nothing happened. When night fell they gathered up their camping gear.

"We go east," Sebastian said.

"What? Iron Lake is west."

"And that's where they're expecting us to go. I've got another rifle in the hummer, and that's east."

"I can't get back, Seb." Mary looked at the darkening skies. "I can't get back onto the Internet."

"I've got a feeling that's not important anymore."

"You're going to leave your rifle behind. You're not one to leave a weapon behind."

"It's what the guy said."

"What?"

"He said to wipe my prints away. Didn't he?"

"Yes. He said that was the only way to save you."

"Do you believe him?"

"I—I don't know. I don't believe anything right now."

"Wipe away my fingerprints . . . why would he say that?"

Sebastian stared out at the dry mountains. He looked at Malone, who grinned at him with his fierce, mouse-big eyes. Malone ready for action.

"This guy you met in hyper space. It wasn't Bobby, was it?"

130

"No. It was someone else. They called him the voice. He's the one in control."

"Well, the one in control doesn't seem to have much control."

"He took my power away. I have no power anymore," Mary said. "I put our story out, and I think I freaked Futurecom out—but I can't go there anymore."

"Where you want to go. Where you want to live."

"Seb, I'm sorry. You can't imagine what it's like being there. Being able to run through hyper space. Being able to find the answer to every question. Being able to know every answer. Being able to move at the speed of light."

"I've seen how you were when you went there," Sebastian said. "You were happy. You were happier than I could have ever made you."

"Now it's over," Mary said.

"So, did you find the answer to every question?"

"No."

They sat together and watched the Utah sun fall into the mountains. Malone posed on a rock like a tiny statue, his ears alert. Mary lay against Sebastian and he rubbed her back. "Is reality so bad?" he asked her.

"Not anymore."

"Don't worry about Mary," the voice said. "Years from now we'll all ask, what became of Mary?"

"Look what she can do."

"She can no longer do anything. The implants have been shut down. Now they're only a couple of dead silicon grains in her brain. They were built to disintegrate when their signals stopped. Her system will absorb them, and eventually she'll pee them out as if they never were."

"So this was all some test?"

"Yes. We needed to see the possibilities tested in the field. When this goes to the Pentagon, I'm going to have to show them that the control chips are reliable; that this is a good piece of equipment for the modern soldier."

"You would have killed her, like Joe, and had her head removed."

"That didn't happen. She found help from the jungle man—and from me."

"You were the one helping her?"

"I didn't want her dead. I didn't want the corporation dead. I'm sorry that two employees died, but they knew what they were signing up for. I never thought Sebastian would turn out so—forceful."

"Love is a pretty powerful force."

"And I'm getting old Sebastian off the hook. It seems a madman named Albert Fletcher shot those two men. His camp was found by the Utah police. The rifle was found, with Fletcher's fingerprints on it, and Mr. Fletcher was found there dead by suicide. Don't worry, he'd already killed himself before we got the body. And the pistol he used."

Carmine shook her head. "What's going to happen to Mary?"

"You ask too many questions. I saved Mary. I saved who I could."

"Why are you telling me this?"

Bobby stared away. "If you want the implants, they're yours. Like Mary, you want to leave this world and go into a world of magic, where you're a goddess. At first it will be like Las Vegas on steroids. But know it will come at a price."

Mary smiled at Malone, who pranced up the rocky slope, excited and proud.

"You love adventure, you little mouse, don't you?"

"Well, he's getting his wish," Sebastian said. He stared into the darkness. "There's a highway just over that ridge."

Mary looked at him. "This isn't where you ditched your hummer."

"No. It would probably be a mistake going back to the hummer."

"So what do we do now?"

"I think it would be wise for us to find some place, an isolated cabin or something, and then lay low for a while. See what happens."

"How are we going to do that?"

"I know places around here. Campsites where cash talks, then keeps its mouth shut."

"We don't have any cash, Seb."

"You don't, maybe. I do. In the bag you've been carrying."

"How much cash?"

"A hundred twenty thousand."

"Good God."

"People like to smoke pot. What can I say?"

"So now we camp out. What can you say? Say that you forgive me, and that you love me."

Sebastian took her into his arms and kissed her. "I'm not going to forgive you for this. And I never stopped loving you."

"Ohhh . . . come on, Malone. We're going to find a cabin."

San Diego Dingo . . . .

I know what you're going to say: another old jerk-weed wants to write about his beloved dog. Important events stalk the earth, and here's another idiot story about somebody's idiot dog. Only a sick sad, lifeless gonad with the retired skinny white legs and grey beard from the 60's would write about his dog.

So, let me tell you about my dog. She's not really a dog, she's a Dingo; and they shoot them in Australia, where they are dangerous pests and roam wild in packs killing and eating lambs (and, but only on rare occasions, children). They're like coyotes, only prettier.

I moved to San Diego, and each day I take Britany to Lake Murray, where she mingles with other dogs. San Diego is the dog loving capital of the world. If I were drowning in Lake Murray, folks here would get out their cell phones and take pictures. If my dog was drowning, they'd make heroic efforts to save her. How much better can it be? As we walk around the lake we confront dogs of every size, shape, breed . . .

Britany lived her whole life on a farm in Nebraska. How is she to react to other dogs, people, and a mind-boggling city surrounding her?

Britany is a very pretty dog. She looks like an over-weight red fox. She's been spayed since birth. Still, she attracts horny male dogs by the pack. My dog knows nothing about sex: she has no idea why the hot male beagle is hopping all over her rump. She puts up with it—and maybe enjoys the strange attention—but gives me a look like, what the hell?

She's clueless, yet something beyond what happened at the vet's makes her grin at the male attention. She smiles like Artemis when I push away a horny wired-haired fox terrier and we go on down the trail. Before I know it, Britany is being humped by a big and aggressive golden retriever that I don't want to mess with.

However, the lady trying to hold back this beast is lovely; in her forties with fetching grey-brown hair, and now completely embarrassed. It's a blue, beaming day, and the sun says that anything's possible.

"Oh, God, Hamlet, no! You get away from her! Stop doing that!"

"This is San Diego," I explain to her, having been here one month. "These things happen." Britany blinks her eyes at me, instinctively letting the big dog rock her world. I wonder if he's thinking 'This bitch is a Dingo, a wild Australian! When am I ever going to get this chance again?'

"Oh, God! I'm sorry!" the woman cries. She wears a straw sunhat, plaid shorts and sandals. Is she here trying to find herself, like me? She yanks the collar of her out-of-control retriever.

"Hamlet! Stop that! Get off her!"

(Hamlet, eh? She reads Shakespeare).

"It's all right," I assure her. "My dog's spayed."

Britany doesn't know what is going on with this slobbering golden retriever; but she's grinning at the attention—does she know?

The lovely woman is wrestling with the big retriever, trying to choke him away from Britany.

"Don't worry about it," I say. "Nothing bad can happen."

"Hamlet, get off her! I'm so sorry! Oh, God—Hamlet—no!"

"Don't worry about it; she doesn't know what it means."

(Unlike me).

I dive into the tryst; we managed to disentangle the dogs, though the horny retriever snapped at me. This is a scene I never saw in my life.

"Hamlet is excited!" I said, getting away from him. Strollers, joggers, walkers, bikers flow by, smirking at the scene. The beautiful woman has got Hamlet locked in his leash; Hamlet stares at my dog with more tragedy than the other guy could do. Dogs seem to express the true, important things. Dogs are elemental souls—why aren't we?

Because we're a bunch of greedy, hateful Dickaloids. Why the hell am I thinking this when the beautiful woman is bending over in a loose San Diego top wrestling with her dog, who is violently in love with the forever-chaste wild Dingo? Could Shakespeare say it any better? I smile at the woman in a creepy elderly way, politely checking out her boobs. My strategy is that I'm old, but not quite dead.

My own dog behaves me, but smiles at the roar she's made; the woman tearing Golden R from her charms. The big golden thing that is barking and grinning and slobbering at her, completely and stupidly in love. Maybe there are some things we can't cut out.

"I should have had him cut," the woman said, brushing a grey-brown strand of hair from her face.

This statement concerned me, but I tried out my charm anyway: "Britany grew up on my farm in Nebraska. So she's not had a lot of experience with other dogs. I sold the farm at a pretty good profit," I added.

The lovely lady has her retriever under control. Now he's only licking Britany's face. "So, you're from Nebraska."

"Lived there all my life." (How much better can a pick-up line be?)

"Oh . . . well, come on, Hamlet, let's go."

"Goodbye," I call. Britany is sniffing at the bushes around Lake Murray—the mint-green scrubs seem to be like cocaine to her nose.

"I moved here!" I call out to the woman.

She smiles behind herself. "I hope to see you again!" she calls.

I lean down to pet Britany, wet with the attentions of the retriever. Other dogs dance around us on their leashes: poodles, pugs, hounds . . . dogs seem to be to San Diego what cows are to Nebraska.

We pass one another on her way back down the trail. She takes Hamlet up the asphalt road, I let Britany take me. She is a lazy dog, and wants very often to not walk—to sniff the strange shrubs that grow along Lake Murray. Living with her in a studio apartment, I'm grateful when she poops and pees at Lake Murray, although I question how romantic I look picking up dog shit in my plastic bag. A sign of responsibility, maybe, but not a page out of Love Story.

The lovely lady smiles going past, even as she is fighting Hamlet against one last jump at my dog.

"Hope to see you again," she says.

"Hope to see you again," I say. "I walk my dog every morning, around nine a.m. Here at the lake."

"That's when I walk Hamlet." She smiles. "So we'll probably see one another again."

"I hope so," I say. "Go Big Red!" (that's a Nebraska line that sometimes works).

"Yeah . . ." She blinks a little back at me; then takes Hamlet away down the path.

Go to Lake Murray one day, if you can. Take your dog. You never know what is going to happen.

Best Friends...

"How the hell did you ever get to be a doctor?"

"I'm smart and everybody around me is stupid. Including you," Dr. Dillard said. "Pull up the gown and let me check your nuts."

"We got the seven o'clock tee-off tomorrow morning. Awwwgh!" Joe shuddered. "This time I'm going to birdie the Ninth and rub the dirty Titlist in your face."

"When shit turns to gold."

"God, this is wrong. Oh, Jesus! How can you do this for a living? I always, Always thought you were gay. Feeling up your best friend's nuts?"

"Hey, after this I'm going to stick my finger up your ass, so quit sniveling. You sniveled in the First Grade and you're still sniveling."

"And I'm the one who protected you from all the bullies who wanted to pound on you for being a know-it-all prick—AWWW!"

"You look ridiculous in that gown." Dr. Dillard laughed. "My God, you look like some mental patient."

"Up your ass."

Dr. Dillard applied a suspicious jelly to his plastic-gloved left hand F-you finger. Dill was left-handed, which only made him more of a dick. Oh, God . . .

"Turn over now and bend over. Okay, now, up yours."

"Oh—God! This is the sickest—Get your fuckin' finger out of there!"

"No sign of cancer in your ass, that's good." Dr. Dillard laughed. Then he frowned. "That little trick you pulled last Saturday . . . ?"

"What?"

"Last Saturday, when you spray-painted that on my bathroom wall, it cost me over a hundred dollars to fix. Dr. Dillard is an asshole, I think that's what it said."

"How do you know I did it?"

"Hey, F—off, asshole! I know it was you who did it."

"You're making big money, you can afford it. Give me a break, I was drunk."

"Hey, fuck you. That stupid spray-painted message really pissed Elizabeth off. It Really Pissed Her Off!"

"I told you not to marry her. OW!"

"Any plumbing problems?"

"What?"

"Like problems with your dick. Any problems pissing or getting it up and finishing the job—not too quickly."

"None of your fucking business."

"I've prescribed enough Viagra to fill a lake."

"No problems, Dr. Dick-ass."

"Okay, now you get your chest X-ray."

"Do we have to go through this every time?"

"Yes, because you're an idiot heavy smoker, and you have been for what—thirty-five years? And I've had to live with the smell of it."

"Let's get this over with."

"I'll mail the X-ray results to you." Dr. Dillard laughed. "You look stupid in that gown."

Joe got his chest X-ray and got back into human clothes. Dill's nurse, Nicole, was a heart-breaker, and he lingered quite a while to flirt with her.

Then he looked down the hall and saw Dill stagger out of his office as if he'd been punched in the stomach. Dill was trying to keep from crying, but he suddenly turned, steadied himself against the wall and wiped tears away, his white doctor's coat heaving and shivering.

Joe's eyes widened. He tried to suspect a joke, but it didn't look like it.

Dill took several deep breaths, shuddered. He turned, and his eyes were shocked to see Joe standing there. He tried to make his face professional. Eyes on the floor, he marched slowly down the hall, the white professional coat moving like an enemy sail. His face was devastated, and he blinked at the floor as if it could do something.

Joe was suspicious, but started to go white. This wasn't the place for Dill to do a joke. He studied his oldest friend. Dill was trying to keep himself together, but he was shaking, and he couldn't look Joe in the eye.

"Okay, good joke. Ha ha."

Dill finally looked up into his eyes. "Joe . . ."

"Come on. What is it? Ha ha from Dr. Fuck. Bad joke."

James Howerton

"No . . ." Dill took a long breath. "I didn't think you'd still be here . . . I thought I could—that I could . . ."

"Okay, not so good joke. What?"

"This isn't a joke."

"What is it? Cancer."

"It's lung cancer."

"This is a joke."

"We need to get another X-ray to be absolutely sure. We'll do it right now."

"This can't be—you couldn't. Come on, Dill. This is a joke!"

Dill stared at the floor. He tried not to cry, but he began crying. "It's not a joke. Let's go, come on. We need another X-ray."

Joe gasped and staggered backward, and Dill grabbed him by the arms to hold him up.

"Tell me this is a joke, Dill."

Dill gave him a scared look. "We'll get you through this."

"Lung cancer." Joe stared at him. "Come on, Dill. This is a joke, right?"

"Joe . . ."

"Is this a joke, Dill?"

"No! God, Joe, this isn't a joke!"

"Okay, okay, well . . ." Joe was suddenly stupid with fear. They stood in silence for long moments, holding onto each other. So strange, the white-and-beige hallway that echoed with nurses and orderlies, some who stared at the two heart-broken friends. "Lung cancer," he said, his voice sounding unreal in his ears.

Dill stared down at the floor. Then he looked up into Joe's eyes. "God, Joe! Jesus God!" He began crying.

142

Joe went white. Dill was trying to hold him up. "Oh God."

"Joe . . ."

"Oh God, Dill. This can't be true."

Dill shook him. "It's not. You don't have cancer, all the tests were fine. It's a joke. But the look on your face!" He broke out laughing.

Joe shuddered and got blood back there. He had to slow his heart and blink at the floor in order to understand the size of this joke. "You—fucking—evil—ASSHOLE! God damn it, Dill! No . . . you can't be that much of a prick."

"You spray-painted my fucking bathroom."

Joe stared at him. "How could you pull such an evil thing? Jesus God Almighty!"

Dill chuckled. "I wanted to scare you into quitting smoking. Don't be such a dick about it."

"Don't be . . . you asshole! I'm going to get you back. And it may be tomorrow, when I try to make a long drive and let the driver slip out of my hands and kill your fuckin' ass. God damn it, that's the most evil thing you've ever done to me, you—fuck!"

"I wanted to scare you into quitting smoking. Stop sniveling about it. Call it payback for writing Dr. Dillard is an asshole on my bathroom wall, in enamel spray paint, where my kids could read it. You should leave it there."

"I should leave it there . . . I should leave it there. It's true, you are a super-asshole. No, you are The super-asshole. No, you're the God of super-assholes. And no, I'm not going to leave it anywhere near there."

"Quit smoking, you dick," Dr. Dillard said. "What part of smoking don't you understand?"

"The part that your ass is mine, Dr . . . . I can't think of a word. There's no human word that can describe what kind of a prick you are. I cannot believe you'd do something like—I'll tell you this, you son-of-a-bitch: pay-back's coming. God, I can't believe you'd . . . lung cancer?"

"The look on your face." Dill laughed.

"Payback's coming, asshole. Payback's coming!"

"We should be even."

"Even . . . are you fuckin' kidding?"

"No. You spray painted my bathroom. Your joke cost me money. My joke didn't cost you a thing."

"Are you fuckin' kidding me!"

"Maybe a little shock and fear, but that only made it funnier."

"Watch your back, Dr. Dick. Tomorrow! I won't tell you what hole it's going to be, maybe even the eighteenth. I get sweaty, and I tend to throw my club at the most evil asshole on earth. Watch your back. Because for that one, it's going to be really bad payback."

"Oh, give me a break. You've been a whiner for thirty years. We should be even."

Joe stared at him. "A professional medical doctor tells me I have lung cancer—my best friend tells me I have lung cancer—God damn, this is way over the top for cruelty."

Dill laughed. "The look on your face."

"Oh, you evil prick. Revenge is going to come swift and—no, that's wrong. It's going to come slow, like some snake sliding up to you. That's how it's going to come, you endless prick. Tomorrow . . . no; whoa, maybe not tomorrow. God damn you to hell, Dill."

Dr. Dillard laughed. "The look on your face," he said.

The Graphite Spider Escapes To Earth...

The Graphite Spider was accused of abusing his Gecks. The charges were true, and so one day he "borrowed" a star ship and streaked away from the center of the galaxy in order to avoid execution.

He chose Earth because it was a baby planet, lost in the vast spiral arms where so many living things existed in an impossible soup of life and stupidity. Also, there were multitudes of organic spiders living here, and—though much larger—he could probably hide out among them. His spacecraft arrived safe, and he programmed it to poof out of existence after he scampered down to his new dirty existence. Now he was stranded.

How tragic that the Graphite Spider had been the greatest chef in the galaxy; he had prepared meals for the Magnificent Oren, Lord of All. Now, to be stranded on this squirmy world, a hiding mechanical being—a criminal.

Well, best to destroy the past because it no longer existed. Best to face reality. Yes, he had abused the Gecks that had served him. They often failed to provide perfect meals for the Lord of All. The Graphite Spider demanded perfection (was this a crime?), and his Gecks had not achieved perfection. He was sure that these same Gecks were now being terminated. Anyway, what were Gecks? They probably didn't even know they were being abused.

It was not the Graphite Spider's fault; and so he got away, in order to avoid persecution, into the swirling mist of stars and planets that hopefully meant nothing to Oren, Lord of All. The Gecks had failed to appease the appetite of the obese God; and the Graphite Spider was damned if he would give his life because those inferior idiots had failed.

Earth was a disgusting, evil place, filled with unaware organic humans who dominated everything with their primitive technologies. In the midst of this, everything squirmed here in a hallucinogenic quagmire of life: things crawled and scampered and galloped and crawled and skittered and slunk and dropped their stinky wastes everywhere. Compared to the electrically sterile plexium kitchen that glittered in the lights of a million planets, this place was already beginning to sicken him, as it would any being from an advanced world.

The perfect place to hide, he had hoped. The Graphite Spider had studied Earth, and Earth humans; not to know them, but to harvest them. When fried with silk-oil from Mulea, they tasted magnificent. The Great Oren belched and farted mightily after human cuisine, a signal that the Graphite Spider would keep his life another day. They were a delicacy, to be sure; but not because they were difficult to harvest. It was because of the great distances that had to be traveled to get here, and the amount of liquid plexium it took, fuel he had acquired, after he had stolen the ship; fuel from Ziggs, the brutal smuggler who charged him everything for it. But what was money now?

"Humans are as tasty," Great Oren had once complimented him, "as the crabs of Coldar and the mushrooms of Singg. You must get me more of them."

"They are very expensive, Sire," said the Graphite Spider.

In better times—oh, to hell with it. That was beside the point. The point now was that the Graphite Spider was stranded here, and may as well make the best of it. He scampered on electric legs into the first hole he could find. He was the largest arachnid form on this planet, but he could retract into himself to become extraordinarily small. If they were truly serious about finding him they would spend the plexium to get here, then cover this world with a magnetic blanket, and if he was scampering on the surface they would find him.

The hole he found was occupied by a fat hairy mammal of some sort, and he electrocuted it with his eyes. Ug. What a disgusting place. He folded himself up and became a quiet graphite ball; safe but certainly not happy in the brown dirt. It may be some time before he could crawl out and re-energize under the bright star that fed this miserable world. Best not to remember the glory of the Hall of Oren. Now was only unfortunate reality.

His eyes glittered hot with the bitterness he felt. He went dormant, and his eyes cooled and he went to sleep. The Graphite Spider was not a saint. He had tortured his Gecks because they simply could not live up to the high standards of their positions. It had been proven that Gecks feel pain, but they were still Gecks. In his sleep he sniffed the dirty, rooty denseness of this world-air.

When he came awake and crawled out of the hole he was in a foul mood. He lay grumping as the powerful star energized him to maximum. His electric eyes danced around, studying the place. The eyes caught on a mass of bushes where berries (some of them fermented), hung purple-black on tired branches. This was indeed a plump world, drunk on itself. The Graphite Spider was an alcoholic, admittedly a mean one, and he eyed the fermented berries with caution.

Ah oh.

Alcohol had caused the problems with the Gecks, and had doomed his relationship with the neon worm-girl from Soo; it was not good when it mixed with his hydraulic oils, and his naturally sour nature. But wait now: stranded on this planet, a fugitive in disgrace, what was there to lose? All charged up, stuffed with the sun, he was the most powerful being on this puny world. Who was to tell him he couldn't get drunk?

And so he gobbled up fermented berries until he was so drunk he staggered on his eight mechanical legs. He stared one-eyed at the planet, cursing his fate, suddenly in rage at everything. He had once been in love with the neon worm-girl who served in the Court of Oren. He thought of her now, where she must be in the vast galaxy, if she had heard of his fate. He hoped bitterly that the next Royal Chef would prove to be a failure, with even worse Gecks.

To hell with everything! The Graphite Spider stumbled into the world, not caring where he was going. To hell with everything—it was all gone, all gone: the celestial palace of Oren, the silver electric kitchen where the incompetent Gecks could not make proper cuisine, the worm-girl who changed color—his love . . .

He stumbled like a broken machine across a sunlit glade. A farmhouse stood nearby, and a female human was raking leaves in her yard. Female humans were very tasty, and Oren the Great had enjoyed them basted in the soft sweet jellies of Manga.

This one was too old and stringy to provide a decent dish. The Graphite Spider stumbled up to her. She saw him, a spider bigger than any she had ever imagined. She freaked, and tried to smash him with her rake. The Graphite Spider electrocuted her with his eyes. The female human collapsed, gasped, clutched at her heart. She wriggled a few moments in the grass yard; then lay still.

I shouldn't have done that, he thought. But she attacked me with a rake. His diamond eyes stared drunkenly, trying to adjust. Forget the neon worm-girl, forget the Magnificent Court of Oren. You are here on this world of dirt. Best now to stay drunk until some kind of plan presents itself. Fermented berries grew everywhere on Earth; no problem getting and staying drunk. The alcohol would eventually dilute his fluids—but to hell with it!

This was a planet dominated by near-monkeys who'd built cities and highways, industries and uncountable stores. The Graphite Spider, so drunk on fermented berries, scampered weirdly to the human house. His drunk brain despised these humans. He had served dominate species all his life, and he was Damned if he would kowtow to these arrogant meat bags.

Like any drunk, the Graphite Spider behaved recklessly. A male human ran out of the farmhouse, seeing his mate dead on the ground. The man knelt down to her, in shock and disbelief. The Graphite Spider stumbled up and zapped him with electric eyes.

Ha ha. Know that I am the most powerful form on this puny planet. Know that you are unaware dirt monkeys in this galaxy.

No matter—no matter at all.

As he watched the male earthling die, an organic Earth spider startled him by dancing out of a hole. There were uncountable insects on this moist world, some which could make interesting stews. Perhaps he would do some culinary experiments here—keep his superior taste senses in shape, to even be able to kneel one day with new and magnificent dishes before Oren the Great.

This Earth spider was a female, and he sensed that she didn't want to try and make him food. Her web glands glistened in the afternoon light. Her global eyeballs studied him warily. She moved on eight stilty legs. She was a bristled, quick-moving thing, with no brain to speak of. Despite his size and strangely mechanical look, smells she sent out told him that she wanted to mate.

Hmmmm . . .

Drunk on Earth berries, the Graphite Spider blinked his electric eyes at her. The female organic spider scampered up to him and presented herself. What the hell, he thought.

When he had spent himself he watched the female spider scamper away. He had planted his seed here on this planet. He had committed a crime, planting on this planet his electric seed. So what? He hadn't escaped here in order to be loveable. It was probably a worse crime electrocuting the humans, as that would draw attention. The other—well, if the girl spider managed to produce his offspring, the damage would be down the road.

The Graphite Spider stumbled back to the fermented berry bush. To hell with everything! He might as well die on this rotten world. He gobbled berries until he passed out, having a last fuzzy thought that he might kill even more of these tall, gawky arrogant apes. Ha ha—who could stop him?

"I'm not Lying!" Stella Amos said. "I'm not crazy and I'm not drunk! It was this huge spider! It was so big I thought it was a raccoon. But it was a spider—like a robot spider."

"A robot spider." Sheriff Klein said.

"Yes!" I went to get my phone and get a picture of it—then Max ran out the dog door and went after it, and these rays came out of its eyes, and Max fell dead!"

"Then what did this big spider do?"

"It went away; it moved real stumbly, like a broken toy or something."

"It moved real stumbly." Sheriff Klein had come here from the Nance place, where Wilma and Royce both lay dead in their back yard from apparent twin heart attacks. He wasn't in the mood for crazy spider stories.

"I tell you now that it was a huge spider, and rays shot out from its eyes and killed Max! It was some kind of robot spider!"

"Mrs. Amos, calm down. A giant spider that shoots death rays out of its eyes?"

This was not a good day for Sheriff Klein.

Nor for the Graphite Spider. He stumbled into a ditch and passed out. He felt the hot Earth star energizing him, but he could feel little else. Hours later he woke up. His head was throbbing and his faceted eyes peered out at a late evening. Many insects had crawled up to him to see if he was dead and might be food.

Ug; what a dirty crawly world this was. The Graphite Spider fried the bugs with his eyes, and stumbled to his feet. He had dreamed in his drunken sleep of the Palace of Great Oren and how the neon worm-girl would smile at him and glow lavender.

Well, he might as well just live with this; but what now?

He stared at a candy red sunset, followed behind by darkness as Earth's star fell below the horizon. The Graphite Spider was still somewhat drunk. His glazed, diamond eyes blinked at reality. He was covered in grit, he stank of this world; and he was somewhat ashamed. He had not escaped here to go on a drunken binge that might get him detected. He bit into one of the ugly beetles he had electrocuted. He was surprised at the taste. It would be a good seasoning for a stew. It would be wonderful if he could harvest the interesting cuisine of this world and return with it in triumph to the Court of Oren. He would never abuse a Geck again. It would be wonderful if Oren had cooled off, had taken on an inferior chef and would welcome him back. He might be able to construct a primitive craft; but there was no liquid plexium on this world. He hadn't thought out his escape; in his terror he had only raced to the most distant primitive planet he could think of. The Great Oren would appreciate—no, best not to think of the Court of Oren out there in the blazing center of the galaxy, it was beyond any dream. The human apeloids couldn't even travel to their nearest star system.

Presently he began to feel sorry for himself. In spite of his better judgment, the Graphite Spider scampered out of the ditch and went down into the creek bed, where the fat fermented berries grew everywhere. In no time he was roaring drunk. He stumbled across a moonlit field. Time to do some exploring.

"They both died of heart attacks," the coroner, Dr. Creighton told Sheriff Klein.

"You're sure, Charlie."

"Yes. There's no doubt."

"That's pretty damn suspicious."

"Well, what probably happened is Wilma was out in the garden; she had a heart attack and went down. Royce saw her out the window, panicked and went running out to the yard to her. That caused his heart attack; they were both on heart medication. I'll admit it's a tragic coincidence—I've never seen it before; but it might not be all that uncommon for a husband and wife at their ages. Anyway, I did a thorough autopsy. It was heart attack, both of them."

Sheriff Klein let it go. No sign of burglary or any other crime; and nobody had a reason to hurt the Nances.

"Stella Amos lost her dog," he mentioned. "Found it dead out in the yard—saw it die, actually."

"Oh; I'm sorry to hear that," Dr. Creighton said. "How'd it die?"

"A robot spider zapped it with a ray."

Dr. Creighton looked at him. "I'm not in the mood for jokes."

"That's what she told me. She calls me, she's frantic; so I stop over there on the way back from the Nance place. She's about as hysterical as I've ever seen a person. Said she saw a giant spider in the yard going over to her plum bushes. The dog, Max, spots it and goes after it. That's when rays came out of its eyes, hit Max, and he fell dead. I'm not joking, Charlie. That is exactly what Stella Amos told me."

"What was she drinking?"

"Didn't appear to be drunk, or on any drugs."

"Maybe she was having a stroke."

"I don't know. She was so upset I had to take her to County General, I guess they'll find out. Then I had to drive back there to get the dog, have it checked for rabies."

"A robot spider . . ."

"That shot death rays out of its eyes."

"You've had a pretty strange day."

Sheriff Klein stared away for a moment. In this quiet county it had been a shock to see Royce and Wilma lying dead out there in the garden.

"I could use a cold one," the sheriff said.

Jose Ramirez was on his way to work—the night shift at the Walmart in Falls City—when his headlights caught the thing scampering across the highway.

His stomach jumped and he slammed on the brakes and stared at it. About the size of a fox, but there was nothing fox about it. It was . . .

He shook his head in disbelief. The giant spider swiveled its head and the lights caught two bulging eyes that sparkled a million colors. This can't be . . .

Suddenly twin beams of white shot into the car, and Jose clutched his chest. As the car rolled slowly into the ditch the Graphite Spider wobbled across the highway and disappeared into the tall grass.

"Another heart attack," Dr. Creighton said. "Don't give me that look—what can I say? He died of a heart attack."

"Did he have heart disease?"

"No history. But I've seen this before. The heart can have a lot of hidden dangers."

"Three heart attacks in two days." Sheriff Klein looked at the floor.

"I don't know what to tell you. Jose Martinez died of a sudden heart attack."

"He wouldn't have felt it coming? Called in sick to work?"

"Not necessarily. It happens."

"There couldn't be some—I don't know—some environmental thing, some chemical thing going on?"

"I don't get you."

"A county this size, and three heart attack deaths in two days, only a couple of miles apart?"

"It's tragic," Dr. Creighton said.

Suddenly Sheriff Klein's radio went off, making them both jump. It was his deputy:

"Sheriff, you ain't going to believe this!"

"What is it, Rollie?"

"Sheriff, we found Jimmy Smith down at the lake . . . he'd been fishing. We found him dead!"

Sheriff Klein stared away at nothing for a long moment. He glanced at Dr. Creighton. Jimmy Smith was what—ten years old?

"What lake?"

"Connestoga. He'd gone down there to fish and his mom called us and we went down there and found him. Jesus God, Sheriff, we tried to get his heart started!"

"What is it?" Dr. Creighton asked.

Klein looked at him. "Maybe another heart attack."

"Sheriff, there ain't no bruises on his body or nothing! There ain't no sign—"

"All right, Rollie, calm down. I'll there in twenty minutes."

He looked at Dr. Creighton.

The fermented berries were sending the Graphite Spider into a tailspin. He could not continue to kill these humans without some consequences; it might not be a wise course staying drunk all the time. He made his way around this lake, staring with stupid eyes at the world he was doomed upon, the nauseating green and brown of it. The young human he had killed would have made a wonderful steak, bathed in balofinich sauce. Spiced just lightly with polan salt. And maybe to soak the flesh in bubbling nijah for a night; then make the unformed bones into a surprise dessert. Then a garnish of Earth beetles, with their crunch and tart flavor . . .

He tried not to think of the neon worm-girl. And he had to stop dreaming of returning to the Court of Oren. He was behaving reckless. Being drunk too much had no doubt contributed to this fate. This should be his wake-up call.

Unfortunately, it wasn't.

Sheriff Klein was getting very sick to his stomach. Even Dr. Creighton, always a calm pragmatist, was green about the gills. He had a very tired and uncomprehending look on his face.

"I guess you know what I'm going to tell you," he said.

The sheriff looked at the floor. "Heart attack."

"It wasn't murder, if that's what you think." Charlie Creighton pushed his glasses to the top of his bald head. "But you might have been right; maybe we ought to contact the CDC in Atlanta."

Klein gave him a grim look.

"Maybe even the EPA. All of these heart attacks occurred within a five mile radius of one another. You might be right; there might be some kind of environmental problem here."

"Charlie, I know I said it, and I thought about it; but this is the middle of nowhere; more cows by far than people. Nothing but pasture and cornfields. There aren't any industrial plants, drug manufacturers, any of that."

"There are chemicals that are known to cause heart attacks; even some toxins that can mask heart attacks, but I had them all checked out. I know what you're thinking, so don't give me that look. I've been County Coroner for forty years. I'll admit, I haven't had to deal with very many questionable fatalities, but none of these deaths is up for discussion. I sent the kid's body to the coroner's office in Lincoln, and they sent it to Omaha. I sent them all the data on Wilma and Royce Nance and

Jose Ramirez. There is no doubt about it: these are All natural heart attacks."

"Massive heart attacks."

"Yes."

"Ramirez had no history of heart issues. Jimmy Smith sure didn't."

"No. That's why—if this isn't some tragic coincidence—we should look into some kind of environmental poisoning. We should have soil tested in that five mile radius; we should have fertilizer and groundwater checked on every farm. I've already sent the Smith boy's body to Atlanta, and the data from the other three; but I know what they're going to tell me."

"Common heart attacks."

"You might want to consider contacting the FBI."

"The FBI; and when they read your data they're going to think I'm a nut job."

"No. Four heart attacks within five miles of each other—in three days! I'll back you to the hilt that this is something that should be checked out; before we have any more."

Any more. Klein chewed at the sides of his cheek, a habit his wife hated, because often it caused bleeding. These couldn't possibly be murders. But if some bad fertilizer or water pollution or other environmental disaster was causing this . . . he blinked his eyes and shook his head. "Charlie, if I brought you the body of a dog, could you tell me the cause of death?"

"A dog. What are you talking about?"

"A dog that fell dead only a half mile from the Nance's."

"Stella's dog. The robot spider story."

"I know I don't have the right to ask you."

"No, no. Bring it in. If it was a heart attack, I'll know it pretty quick."

Am I going mad? Klein asked himself.

Am I going mad? The Graphite Spider asked himself.

No. He was drunk, but not mad. His sensory radar detected the magnetic field that was falling mildly over the skies, like a harmless static. He lurched as best he could into a nearby hole, where he electrocuted another fat burrowing mammal that snarled at him. There he lay terrified, waiting for a signal he knew was going to come.

He felt sick all at once.

He could sense them closing in up there, and he wished he had not eaten the fermented berries, nor zapped those humans.

I wouldn't have mattered: if Oren had commanded assassins to come after him, it was probably because he had stolen the ship and bought illegal liquid plexium from Ziggs, who might already be dead. How drunkenly stupid to think you could escape an angry God like Oren. He lay shuddering in the dirt hole, his sensors listening to the crackling signal of the magnetic blanket overhead, waiting for the voice to come to him.

They were close.

"The collie died of a heart attack," Dr. Creighton said. "So whatever is killing people is killing dogs too. It's got to be environmental."

Sheriff Klein had to agree; but in the back of his exhausted mind, he thought . . . no.

"I need to get this information out to the folks of this county," he said. "You on board with that?"

"Yes."

"They already know something real bad is happening. Until the high muckety mucks get their asses down here and start testing, folks should know that we're very concerned about these heart attacks—that you know as well as I do are not Natural! They might not be murder, as we know it, but this sure as hell isn't natural. So you're going to back me up on this?"

Dr. Creighton thought of the dog, strangely enough. "Yes," he said.

Now came the voice in his electronic head that the Graphite Spider had been dreading to hear, while he desperately tried to sober up:

We will find you. You know this.

It was the voice of a god damned Geck. Oren had sent Gecks after him; and why should that surprise him, considering the crime he'd been charged with? Assassins fitting the crime; and a way of giving the Graphite Spider a last full dose of shame and justice. The Graphite Spider's senses sparked as he heard:

Oren does not want you dead—yet. We will find you; you know this.

The Graphite Spider desperately tried to drag his mind out of the fermented berries and make considerations: Oren had spent a star ship and liquid plexium to find him; He meant business. This was a ploy to draw him into the open so the Gecks could kill him. It would be a pleasure for them, after his reputation among them had been revealed. Or was it Oren luring him home so that the obese God could make his death slow and incomprehensible in the Agony Chamber, for the benefit of his court (and a message to them)?

Or could it be true; Oren forgave him, and his exile on this filthy world was enough punishment and Oren wanted him back and he could go back and bow and beg forgiveness and forgiveness would be granted and Oren would command him to make a feast as only he could and to forever stay away from drunkenness and the Graphite Spider would promise and retire into the glorious plexium kitchen to bask in his marvels and maybe even the neon worm-girl . .

It was obviously a moment of truth, and the Graphite Spider wished he weren't so thoroughly stinking drunk. His glittering eyes blinked in the blackness of this dirt hole. He could maybe avoid capture, but it was doubtful. Oren would send Gecks practiced in the cruel art of finding and killing criminals on any planet in any environment. The Graphite Spider was an alcoholic chef. And if he could manage to escape them and they gave up, would it be any kind of life here, on this place?

Still, what humiliation being executed by a lowly Geck (and it would be like Oren to order such a thing). His reputation, his fame and character would forever be despised. Lithium creatures would spit acid at the sound of his name—if Oren ever let it be spoken again. And what would the neon worm-girl think? What would she feel? She had never even suspected that he was an alcoholic.

He blinked his eyes, sighed and smelled the overwhelming odor of this dirty water world. Worm things with no brains at all crawled out of the ground around him; and bugs he didn't dare electrocute, or risk detection from above.

Better to have died back at the Court; better not to have stolen a ship and plexium and tried to escape here. He was doomed. His eyes blinked at the darkness one last time; then he sent a signal upward with his brain, toward the magnetic field.

This was a wise choice, the voice of the Geck said in his brain. It sounded disappointed, and the Graphite Spider saw some spark of hope.

Come into the open and keep your signal on until we arrive.

The Graphite Spider loathed taking orders from a Geck; but he crawled out of the hole and finally did what he was told. Soon enough he felt a tornado of magnetism fall down upon him, lifting him there into the invisible ship.

Now I will die, he thought.

"Well, they're sending some guys out from the university in Lincoln to do some tests," Sheriff Klein said.

"What about the federal government?"

"They said they studied your coroner's reports. They don't see anything at present to suggest this is anything but a coincidence."

"So we're two Chicken Littles," Charlie said.

"Right now we are."

"Right now."

"We might not have seen the last of this. It just feels wrong."

"You're not going to kill me?" he asked the head Geck when he was in custody.

No, sadly enough.

"Then you'll take me back and Oren will put me in the Agony Chamber."

The Geck shrugged. *We can only hope so. But who knows the mind of the Great Oren? I think not, though. I think you are unjustly a very lucky creature.*

The Graphite Spider blinked his drunken eyes. "You think not. What are you saying?"

Great Oren acquired three chefs in your absence, none of whom proved satisfactory. He misses your cooking.

The Head Geck gave him a disgusted look. *But we do not go directly back. We must stay here for a little time.*

"Stay here on Earth—why?"

Oren commands you to harvest as many humans as the ship will carry. He seems obsessed with them.

The Graphite Spider tried to get his thoughts around this miracle. If Oren wanted him in the Agony Chamber, what could he do about it now? Like any drunk, his mood shifted quick from despair to arrogance. "He's obsessed with them because of the way I cook them." The Graphite Spider gave one eyeball of contempt to the Head Geck, believing that this, his most desperate dream, was coming true. The little spark of hope burst into a glorious flame.

"I tell Him good jokes," the Graphite Spider said to the Geck. "Do you often entertain Him?"

No, I do not. I have never seen The Emperor.

"Well, then stop standing there giving me your insolent look. There are humans to harvest—and you will do exactly as I tell you. We will stock this ship as fat as we can, but we have to leave room for spices.

Lord Oren never spoke of spices.

"Don't question me or I'll have You in the Agony Chamber. Insects! Don't look at me like that; you know less than nothing about food and how to prepare it, so simply do as you're told. We'll have to collect as many as we can. I'll show your crew how to do it quickly, if they're not too stupid to learn."

The Head Geck was staring at him in pure hatred, knowing he was drunk. *The Great Oren said nothing of insect spices—*

"Keep your mouth shut," snapped the Graphite Spider. "We'll make room for these spices if we have to push some of your crew out of the door. Do you understand me?"

The Geck said nothing, only stared at him with a stiff face.

"Do you understand me?" the Graphite Spider repeated. "And we must make room for a load of certain fermented berries. Surely some of your crew are expendable."

Fermented berries . . .

And no random killing of humans, that would be foolish. I'll find the ones to be harvested. I will give the orders. Is this understood?"

The Head Geck glared at him in hatred (Ha ha!), but nodded and said, *It is understood.*

"There is a place near here where we can harvest the best humans. Steer the ship that way, and try not to be stupid."

Sheriff Klein's stomach would not be comforted with four Tums. Somehow he felt a terrible thing falling down over his county like a dark quilt. Maybe it was exhaustion; maybe it was seeing so much sudden death at once. He knew Charlie was getting paler and greyer under the strain.

He looked up from the floor. "We either made asses of ourselves, or something bad is going on."

"Maybe it is just a coincidence," Creighton said. "That's where all the evidence—tragic as it is—points. No toxins were found in any of the bodies, no sign of pollutants, no elevated signs anywhere that would suggest anything else."

"I hope we made asses of ourselves."

Klein's phone went off, and his stomach burst into fire: "Sheriff Klein."

The voice made him shudder: "Sheriff, get down here!" Rollie's voice. "Sheriff, get everybody and everything down here! We need people—paramedics, nurses, all that! Sheriff, get everybody down here!"

"Rollie, calm down. Get everybody where?"

"Walnut Middle School."

Call Me Darkness . . .

I don't know how the guy got my number. I picked up the phone and here was this distorted voice wanting to discuss a matter of protection that would only cost me a hundred grand.

I had to laugh: I'm the guy who gets paid for protection.

I laughed at first.

"Who the hell is this? You sound like a fucking robot."

"Call me Darkness. I can't stay on the line long," this Darkness voice said. "So listen fast and careful. I'm a sniper; I think I'm one of the best in the world, and I'm offering you the deal of your life."

"What—"

"No, just listen. Pay me 100 thousand dollars and I'll go away forever. I'll be out of your life and you'll be a very smart man. I'll give you instructions how to get the money into an account—"

"Fuck you. What kind of fucking joke is this?"

"If you refuse this deal," the robot said. "One of your guys will get shot in the head."

"What the fuck joke—Tommy, is that you? Okay, I get it, good joke, you fucking pricks."

"This isn't a joke. I'm not Tommy. One of your people will die of you don't pay me 100 thousand dollars right now. Then each time I kill one of you the price doubles. So it's 100 now, or 200 later, and you lose one of your crew. And so on."

I couldn't believe my ears. "You know who the fuck you're talking to, psycho? How'd you get my private number?"

"I'm very good. And I know who I'm talking to. Don't pass up this first offer, or one of your pals will die. Believe me, down the road—"

"Hey, fuckstick! Down the road? Hey, you try to fuck with me, down the road I'll feed your balls to my fucking pit bull."

"You don't have a pit bull; you have a poodle—at least your wife does."

"What the fuck—"

"Listen to me," the robot said. "Because down the road you're going to find that this is important: it's simple. One hundred thousand now or I start killing you off; each time one of you dies the price doubles. If it reaches a million, you'll be the one to get it."

"Fuck you, psycho." I shut off the phone. No i.d., no call back number. Might have came from an old-fashioned land line. It wasn't a joke the fellas were playing on me, they didn't want their knees snapped. I wondered if De Angelo was behind this, if he'd sniffed out our big C shipment and wanted to put some kind of squeeze on me. This didn't smell like De Angelo, though. I thought about telling the fellas, but no. I didn't want no distractions while this C deal was going down. The guy had my private number (my wife don't even get that), and he knew about Fifi. That meant the prick knew my address.

Two nights later Tommy called me with the news: Carl, Sammy and Paul were leaving the Chico Club at about eleven. Then Carl fell down in the parking lot. They thought he tripped; then they thought he was having a heart attack, because he started twitching and spazzing. Then they saw the bullet hole in his head.

"We didn't even hear nothing," Paul said to me on the phone. "Shot in the head and we didn't hear no fucking gun shot. Then fucking cops everywhere. We didn't even know what direction it came from. Who the fuck would want to shoot Carl?"

My belly turned. "Carl's dead," I heard myself say. God damn you, De Angelo. Carl was the point man on this C deal; now Tommy was gonna have to step up—or me.

That's when the nightmare started. That's when my private phone scared the shit out of me and on the other end was the robot:

"I warned you."

"You cocksucker! I'm gonna find you real fast. And if the cops find you first, that won't matter. All that means is you'll get it in the pen instead of the street. I'll cut you up into dog meat, you prick!"

"No, you won't."

"It don't matter if the cops find you first. I got ways, motherfucker—I got ways."

"No, you don't. I warned you and you didn't listen. That got Carl Salvi dead. Now you owe me 200, or another of you goes down. I think I've proven myself, so please don't go stupid on this. I don't like killing people, even turd-bags like you. 200 is the best deal of your life. Now you know what I can do."

"You're fucking crazy."

"You're going to get another of your people killed thinking like that; then the price goes up to 400 thousand. Carl's dead. Don't go any farther down this road—not with me."

My stomach burned like a fucking volcano. "I'll kill you."

"No. You'll get your people killed if you go stupid on this. You might get lucky and get me, or the cops might get me; but I doubt it. I'm very good. 200 thousand here and now, and I vanish and you'll never hear my voice again."

"Are you working for De Angelo, you cocksucker?"

"Yes, I am."

"You're lying."

"Pay me now and I'll go after De Angelo next. I'm offering you a way out of this."

I thought about it, I won't lie. I'd been strong-armed before—but not like this. Carl was dead, and Sammy and Paul right next to him didn't even know it happened.

"I need to talk to my people," I said.

"How much time?"

"Couple of days."

"One day," said the voice. "Then I'll call you; and if you don't pay the 200 thousand, another one of you will die and the price for getting rid of me will be 400 thousand."

"Fuck you."

The phone went dead. I thought about Carl; then I got on the phone to Tommy, Sammy and Paul. Emergency meeting at the Chico Club. Jesus, some shit like this when the C's coming!

"Well, that's what it is," I said. "The prick wants 200 G, or he says one of us gets what Carl got. Then it goes up to 400."

"Jesus Christ," Paul said. "Who is this cocksucker?"

"I don't know. He told me to call him Darkness."

"Some guy from De Angelo," Sammy said.

"Some guy he brought in," Paul agreed.

We kept our mouths shut when Suzi the waitress came in to fill the drinks. We were gonna need the drinks tonight. I tipped her a twenty and told her to keep them coming. She gave me that smile of hers; but don't get me wrong: it wasn't the kind of smile a hooker gives you, or a stripper when you're flashing cash. Suzi had a fresh smile; and around this place that was pretty fucking rare. I watched her walk out of the private room, and I remembered that body of hers.

"You ain't saying we're gonna pay this cocksucker," Tommy said. "We pay some fucking voice on the phone 200 grand or he'll shoot us?"

"That's what he says. He might be some special hire of De Angelo's, I don't know. But look what he did to Carl—and you guys didn't even hear the gun go off. He tells me he's a very good sniper. Carl gets shot in the head, and you think he tripped? That sounds like a pretty fucking good sniper."

"Fuck him," Tommy said. "We put a tag on this prick. We send Mancini after him."

"We pay this guy off," Paul said. "How's it gonna look?"

"Specially if he's one of De Angelo's."

That was the thing. We pay this guy and show that we're weak, what's to keep him from coming back for more. That's how it works.

"We got tonight to decide," I said. "Then he says another one of us goes down, and it bumps up to 400 thousand."

"Fuck him," Tommy said. "I ain't giving this prick a dime."

He did give Suzi a twenty tip when she came into the private room to fill us back up, and I didn't like that. She patted me on the shoulder as she was leaving, and gave me that smile.

"We pay this cocksucker," Sammy said. "He comes back for more—you know that. And De Angelo knows every time he brings the prick back in he can squeeze our balls."

"Paul? What do you think?"

"It can't be a coincidence that this comes down right before the shipment. De Angelo must have sniffed us out."

We all got quiet at this. Paul had dropped a hint that all of us read. This was where you didn't dare trust even your best friends. Whoever this darkness prick was, he knew who we were, so he had to be somewhere inside. The problem was, I didn't think it was De Angelo—it just didn't smell like him. I had the bad feeling that this was some guy from nowhere, who did his homework, was a good sniper, and could do what he already proved he could do.

"So here's the deal," I told them. "The guy's gonna be calling me tomorrow for an answer."

We shut up when Suzi came in and freshed us up with Chivas clean. I tipped her twenty. When she was gone I gave the guys the look. "The prick showed what he can do," I said.

"Put Mancini on his ass," said Sammy. He looked at Tommy and they both nodded. That worried me, cuz there's a point in our game when you don't trust nobody. All I knew was that Carl was in the ground.

"Okay, you know the story," I said. "A vote."

"Tell him to go fuck himself," Tommy said. He'd made a point of staring at Suzi's ass when she left. Now he wanted to be Mr. Tough.

"Sammy?"

"Let the cops get him. Murder's murder. We can deal with him when he's in the pen."

"Paul?"

I wanted Paul's take because he figured things and didn't just automatically go all stupid and macho. Paul was going to say something; then he went dead.

"He took out Carl like a light bulb," I said. "Carl gets his head shot off, you don't hear nothing—you don't even know it happened."

"I didn't hear nothing," Paul said. "I didn't see nothing. All the sudden Carl's dead."

"We can't underestimate this prick," I said. "He proved what he can do. And he says if we pay him off, he'll go after De Angelo next."

"You can't believe this fuck," Tommy said. "We pay him 200 and you think he's going away? He ain't going nowhere."

"And we're the puss on the block, with our biggest score of C coming in." Sammy began playing with his Rolex, a habit that always irritated me. "Send Mancini after this prick," he said.

"Mancini's expensive," Paul said. "Two hundred's a kick in the balls—but this guy proved what he can do."

"The cops'll get him," Sammy said. But he was playing with his Rolex. Sammy always played with his fucking Rolex when he got nervous. That's what made him a bad poker player.

"Okay," I said. "When the prick calls, what do I tell him? Your vote, Paul. Tell him to go fuck himself?"

"We gotta go there. Yeah, tell him to go fuck himself."

"Okay."

When the phone went off, I'll admit my stomach acted up. I had the instinct that this was right out of nowhere—and that robot voice . . . you'd be a little freaked out too:

"It's Darkness," the robot said.

"I'm here," my voice said.

"Are you ready for the instructions on wiring the money?"

"200 grand, eh?" I said. "Then you keep coming back for more."

"Don't do this," the robot said. "The next friend you lose is going to push it up to 400 thousand. And then on to 800."

I felt sick, but it's the way it is. "We give you the 200, what's to keep you coming back for more?"

"You think I like this? No, 200 is plenty, then I go after De Angelo. I leave Tommy, Sammy, Paul and Louie alone."

He knew who we were. I had a moment where—but no, we had our vote.

"Go fuck yourself," I said.

Tommy got it in the head in his own front yard. He was playing with his dog. The sniper got him and now things went crazy: things got serious. Cops everywhere, all over this; news reporters, cameras, even the feds. In the middle of the C coming in, this was bad. I didn't sit on my dead ass. I had cop friends and even fed friends. I fed them my take, that this was De Angelo's work—but they didn't think so, and I didn't either. This didn't smell like De Angelo—he ain't this good.

I started to know that this was a practiced professional—I didn't know if it was De Angelo's guy or not. Jesus, Tommy was dead! Carl and now Tommy! Both of them out of nowhere, blasted in the head.

And when the phone call came, it'd be 400 thousand.

And it was: "Don't get suicidal over this," the robot said. "Four hundred thousand is do-able, you know? Very cheap if you don't want to die. I won't stay on the line long."

"You fucking prick. You think you can buy me off?"

"Yes, I do." The phone went dead.

At Tommy's funeral I took Sammy and Paul aside: "He called me. This time he wants 400."

They gave me the look, but it is what it is. They saw Tommy dead as dirt. Paul stared at the ground. Sammy played with his Rolex.

"Carl got sniped out of nowhere, Tommy got sniped. This guy is what he said he is."

"You think 400's going to make him go away?" Sammy said.

"I think it might."

"What? No, fuck this. Send Mancini after his ass."

"Mancini's expensive," Paul said.

"We gotta go after De Angelo. Hit him where he's hitting us."

"We got that C coming in," I reminded them. "Last thing we need is more publicity—more cops, the feds."

"It can't be long before they get this cocksucker," Sammy said.

I had friends in the feds; and I had cops in my pocket. News people wouldn't have worried me so much—but we had this big C coming down; and now two of my best were down in the dirt.

"Let the feds get this guy." Sammy was about to tear his Rolex apart.

"How's De Angelo gonna take that?" Sammy said.

"It'd be a bad message," Paul said. "But how they gonna know if we pay the prick off?"

"Cuz he's one of De Angelo's guys."

"I don't think he is," I said. "De Angelo's not that smart, and he ain't that stupid. He don't want the cops and feds and news any more than we do. They're jumping on him more than us, cuz it's our people getting popped."

Sammy seemed to be talking to his Rolex: "We pay the 400, that's gone money?"

"Probably."

"Fuck that."

"This guy knows what he's doing," I said. "Whoever he is, De Angelo's guy or not, we can't have this with the C coming in. Tommy's dead, Carl's dead—we gotta play the cards we got dealt. This prick calls me, I'm paying him off. You guys don't want to pony up, I'll cover you."

I gave a special look to Sammy. He knew that if I covered him I'd never trust him again. As he twisted his god damn Rolex, I knew that he was wondering if I was behind this, trying to squeeze money. That's the game we play—you don't trust your grandma.

"I'll cover you," I said.

"Then the prick comes back for more."

"If he does, we try and handle him from there. I don't think he'll come back, because I don't think this guy's stupid. I think he'll go after De Angelo next. Anyway, I'm paying up. The guy proved himself. Every time he sits and waits with his rifle he's risking his life. Paul, you in with this?"

"Yeah, I'll pony up. I don't like it, but this guy's busted our balls; now Tommy and Carl are dead—and we got all that C coming in."

"Okay. You don't want to pony up a share, Sammy, I'll cover you."

"We let this prick take our money and our respect—"

"Sammy! This ain't about respect—okay? It's about not getting popped in the head one day. We pull the C off, we'll cover the dough."

Suzi came in and freshed up the drinks. I didn't like how Sammy looked at her and tossed her a twenty like she was some kind of stripper. I'd cover Sammy on this;

but I'd never trust him again, him and his fucking Rolex that he played with like it was his dick.

"When he calls I'm gonna pay him off," I said.

"Then the prick's gonna come back for more."

"Don't worry about it, Sammy; I'll cover you."

Sammy wasn't that stupid; he knew what I meant. "What about Mancini. He can find this prick."

"The feds can't find him, Mancini ain't gonna find him. And Mancini ain't going near this."

"You think we pay him off," Paul said. "He's going after De Angelo?"

"I don't know. But he calls, I'm paying the 400."

"And that's gone money."

"Probably. This guy's got us figured out, he's gonna have the money figured out. That's what it is." I threw my hands up—what more could I do?

"I'll pony my share of 400," Sammy said. "But this is fucked up."

"It's fucked up," Paul said. "But he goes after De Angelo next, it might be a good deal. And we got that C on the way."

I waited for the phone to go off, and finally it did:

"Are you ready to wire the money?" the robot asked.

"Yeah. Tell me what to do."

"You have a pen? Ready to write this down?"

"Yeah."

I wired the money out of my account and fast as that it was gone, into some money-go-round that even the feds couldn't probably trace. The 400 thousand wasn't coming back; but money could always be made. Money ain't doing Carl no good, or Tommy. All that mattered was the Darkness might now go away.

"Okay," I said into the phone. "Now you go after De Angelo?"

"I'll stop coming after you."

The phone went dead, and I had the feeling I'd never hear the fucking robot again. Now it was to get the C unloaded and hope for the best. The phone never rang again, and we got the C in and everything went okay. We made the 400 back and then some. I hoped the Darkness'd go after De Angelo like he said he would—but he didn't. He disappeared. What are you gonna do?

I went to the Chico Club, where Sammy and Paul were getting drunk celebrating the C that came in safe. I got a clean Chivas from some fag waiter who was new.

"Where's Suzi?" I said.

"Suzi quit. She wanted to get out of the city."

The guy was so faggy he couldn't even say his esses. "Suzi left."

"What—Suzi left?" Sammy squeezed his Rolex, and I didn't like it. "Where'd she go?"

"No idea," the fag waiter said. "Can I get your order, Sir?"

"She took a bus—what?"

"I really don't know. I guess a rich relative died and she inherited some money."

"How much money?" I asked him.

"I don't know, Sir. Can I take your orders?"

"Chivas clean, all round. What did she say?"

"Suzi? I don't think she said anything."

I stared down at the floor. What I didn't like about the Chico Club was the fucking giant mirror behind the bar. The private room was safe, but it depressed the shit out of me, especially now that Suzi was gone. Here in the main room you couldn't sit no fucking where without seeing yourself in that fucking mirror. I had it installed there so you could sit at the bar and see if anybody was coming up behind you; all I ever saw was myself, and Suzi as she walked in a kind of floating way. Things were okay money-wise, but it hit me that Suzi just took off without even calling me.

"Stop with the fucking Rolex, Sammy!" I snapped.

"What?"

I didn't like that fucking mirror, where you had to see yourself all the time.

"You playing with that fucking watch all the time. It fucking irritates the shit out of me!"

Sammy looked at me for a bit: "So when's the prick going after De Angelo?"

"He might not."

"So we tossed 400 away."

"We got the C," Paul said. "We're still sitting good."

"Without Carl and Tommy," I said. "Stop with the fucking Rolex!" I said to Sammy. "What the fuck is with you and that fucking watch?"

"I'm gonna miss Suzi," he said. "She loved this Rolex. I might have given it to her."

Sammy was about as dumb as shit. He gave me a look: "What, now we have to get our booze from fag-man who has a fag lisp?" he said to me.

"I miss her too," Paul said, shooting down his drink. "But get over it." Paul looked at me. "Broads come and they go."

Suzi was different. I don't love my wife; I don't love these guys. Love's for pussies. If I ever got close to love it was with Suzi.

The fag filled our drinks, and I thought about Suzi, and how 400 grand could get you anywhere, if you're that smart and that good.

"You don't even know where she went?" Sammy asked the fag. "Suzi."

"I don't know, Sir."

"Suzi found her way out of the darkness," I said.

THE END